Sinderella Sexy

Jan Springer

Published by Spunky Girl Publishing, 2015.

Also by Jan Springer

Pleasure Bound
A Hero's Welcome
A Hero Escapes
A Hero Betrayed
A Hero's Kiss
A Hero Wanted
Captive Heroes

Pleasure Bound Boxed Set
Pleasure Bound : COMPLETE SERIES SciFi Erotic Romance Boxed
Set

Tentacles Shifter Erotic Romance
Taken by Him

The Key Club
A Merry Menage Christmas
Sophie's Menage
Jewel's Menage
Jaxie's Menage

The Outlaw Lovers
Jude Outlaw
The Claiming

Colter's Revenge
Tyler's Woman
Resistance
The Outlaw Lovers
Alpha Outlaws Boxed Set

Vampira
Sweet Heat
Dark Heat
Wet Heat
Crimson Heat

Standalone
A Touch of Menage Boxed Set
Shades of Menage Boxed Set
Nice Girl Naughty
Sinderella Sexy
The Biker and The Bride
The Fire Within
Bared to Him
Pleasure Bound : A Futuristic Adult Romance Boxed Set
Merry Menage Kisses Boxed Set
Inner Girl Rising
Stripped Naked
Risqué Girl Delights Boxed Set
A Holiday Menage
Ménage À Trois
A Hitman for Hannah
Billionaire Boyfriend
Edible Delights

Vampira
Toygasm
The Dark Side

Watch for more at www.janspringer.com.

Sinderella Sexy
Jan Springer
By day, she's a dedicated gynecologist.
By night, Dr. Ella Cinder, escapes reality by secretly performing in her own version of Cinderella, aptly re-titled Sinderella.

When sexy colleague Dr. Roarke Stephenson shows up in the Sinderella audience on the same night her Prince Charming stands her up, Ella seizes the opportunity to make Roarke into her Prince Charming for one carnal night of extremely naughty fun in front of an audience.

But at the strike of midnight, Ella knows she must face the harsh reality that Roarke must never learn her secret life and they can never be together again. Until then, she'll make sure he'll never forget their night of sensual play.

Dr. Roarke Stephenson is immediately captured by the lusciously curvy actress who hides behind a mask and is known only as Sinderella. For some insane reason she reminds him of his klutzy co-worker, Ella. But that's not possible. Ella would never have the nerve to do the wickedly delicious things Sinderella does to him, or would she?

Trademarks Acknowledgement
The author acknowledges the trademarked status and trademark owners of the following wordmarks mentioned in this work of fiction:
Velcro: Velcro Industries B.V. Limited Liability Company

1

Sinderella Sexy

Published by Spunky Girl Publishing
Copyright 2015 Jan Springer
2nd edition
Cover Art by Talina Perkins of Bookin' It Designs
Edited by Amelia S. Black

Chapter One

DESPERATION GRIPPED Ella as she lay bound and naked on the gynecologist's examination table. A fine sheen of perspiration laced her skin. Her hips undulated as Roarke penetrated her with the dual vibrator, creating incredible sexual tension. The rhythmic motions of the thrusts made her body hum, pulse, ache for release.

He'd kept her on the edge for so long, she could barely think straight.

"I've wanted to do this to you since the first day I met you, Ella," he said. His deep voice smoothed over her flushed skin like a jolt of lightning.

"You want more, Ella?" he purred.

Excitement flared like a firecracker. She trembled with anticipation.

She could barely see him through the sexual haze. Could hardly see his sparkling, lust-filled green eyes or the sexy smile he reserved only for her.

Hurry!

She wanted *him*, not the freaking vibrator!

"I want you," she pleaded hoarsely, and thrashed her head back and forth. She needed to come so bad. Needed release or she would simply go mad with desire.

"Please, Roarke, please make love to me," she whimpered.

"And so you shall have me, Ella," he said hoarsely. His face twisted with sexual hunger. His eyes glazed with lust. "You shall have my big cock deep inside your tight little pussy—"

"Good morning, sorry I'm late," Dr. Roarke Stephenson's deep, masculine voice slammed into Dr. Ella Cinder's fantasy like a sensual punch, making her suck in her breath and spill her coffee onto the elaborate oak conference table.

"Christ, Ella! You're such a damn loser!" her stepmother's harsh whisper made Ella flinch and she quickly threw a pile of napkins over the puddle of steaming coffee.

Her face flamed as her two stepsisters; Drs. Wanda and Manda Cinder elbowed each other gleefully and chuckled snidely beside her.

Bitches! Ella thought as she pushed against the bridge of her black-framed glasses in order to keep them from falling off her nose while she wiped at the steaming coffee. From the corner of her eye, she spied the man of her frequent sexual fantasies stroll into the room.

He scowled at her stepmother, obviously overhearing her rude remark, but thankfully, he said nothing. Roarke was still relatively new and she didn't want him getting into trouble on her account.

When he passed by, his delicious male scent slammed into her with such a wicked force her senses spiraled into sexual awareness mode.

Oh, my! He always looked so damned sexy. He wore the traditional white lab coat fully opened, revealing a light green shirt that stretched across his big chest as well as a pair of tight jeans that cradled his awesomely huge bulge. With his short brown hair and a shadowy stubble covering his strong jaw, he looked more like a dangerous bad boy than a prestigious gynecologist.

He sat down beside her and she noted his lust-sparkling gaze slide over her in one hot wave making her entire body tighten with need.

Her self-control, or at least what was left of it, crumbled as visions of her most recent fantasy invaded her thoughts again. Their naked bodies fused. The scent of their sex hanging heavy in the air. His long, thick cock pushing deep inside her wet, hungry vagina.

Her pussy creamed in reaction.

She had to stop fantasizing about the sexy doctor. She had a bad habit of daydreaming about him whenever she felt overworked and tired...which was pretty much all the time. Overworked because she accepted twice the number of patients than any other doctor in the hospital did at the same wage they got, and tired because of her deliciously naughty nighttime activities. Activities that made her fantasize about Roarke day and night.

Was it any wonder whenever he came near her she felt so nervous and flustered that she became all thumbs?

The last thing she wanted to do was to appear incompetent in front of her fellow gynecologists. Especially when she needed them for the occasional problem cases she snuck into the consultation pile, just like the one she'd boldly plopped onto the pile today. She didn't want her patient to suffer any longer, and had decided to bite the bullet and seek the second signature required as per Cinder policy for giving medication without awaiting the lab results to confirm her suspicions.

"You really should cut down on all that daydreaming, Ella," her much too thin stepsister Manda rolled her eyes with disgust. Then she scrunched her skinny lips in an unattractive grimace as she looked at the pile of donuts set on a crystal plate in the middle of the conference table.

"It's not her daydreaming. The klutz simply drinks too much coffee," her other stepsister Wanda chuckled as she heaved her large frame out of her chair and picked up her fourth chocolate-dipped donut.

Ella sighed wearily as their comments needled into her heart. By now, she should be immune to their rudeness. Yet she wasn't. Compliments of her oversensitive nature, she supposed.

What in the world had she done to deserve such a horrid stepfamily anyway?

"Doctors, please. Let's not show our immaturity so early in the morning," Roarke grumbled as he poured some coffee and grabbed a donut. To Ella's surprise, he winked at her.

Oh sweet mercy! Roarke winked at her, and she was gushing back at him like a silly schoolgirl.

"Oh for crying out loud, Ella. Hurry up and clean the mess so we can get on with today's caseload. We're already ten minutes behind schedule," her stepmother huffed. Disgust flashed on her wrinkled face and her three chins wobbled as she also grabbed herself a donut.

Ella bit back a sharp retort. She wished she could just tell them where to stick their donuts and their snide remarks. One of these days, she would do just that. Not today though. Today she needed their help.

"So tell me about this latest problem case you're working on? This girl named China Smith." Roarke suddenly asked. She hadn't even noticed he'd started reading the file.

Ella stopped wiping the table. Ignoring the irritated looks of her stepsisters and stepmother, she relished the familiar pounding of adrenaline that roared through her system. This time it wasn't the usual sexual energy she felt whenever she thought of Roarke, but the energy of living on the edge with these complicated pregnancy cases she had a tendency of taking on.

"Her symptoms include a rash, a stiff neck, blood in her mouth, seizures, to name a few," Ella replied in a rush, hoping her stepfamily wouldn't interfere just yet with their embarrassing protests. "I've done the appropriate tests to rule out stomach cancer, sepsis, meningitis, checked for intracranial bleeding—"

"What do you know about her personal life?" he asked softly. His gaze held hers and Ella took yet another deep breath to steady her nerves. Was that concern in Roarke's eyes? Or was he deliberately prodding her for more information so her stepfamily could gloat when they shot her down. No, he wouldn't intentionally hurt her.

Although there was nothing she could put her finger on, she sensed there was a gentle side to this confident man. A side he kept well hidden. Up until now, he fit in here quite nicely, thinking only in dollars and cents and taking in wealthy clients who would benefit the hospital. Perfect Cinder material, her stepmother had cooed after they'd interviewed him several months ago. Perfect husband material, her stepsisters had whispered.

Ella had been smitten with him too. Wishing and dreaming that she would one day have this handsome, confident, rich doctor for her very own. Unfortunately, her dreams and wishes had died a cruel death when she'd seen the photograph of him and his fiancée in his office shortly after he'd been hired.

Over the months, he'd appeared quite the professional with her. Those heated looks she caught him throwing her way were probably just her imagination, but they'd ignited erotic fantasies that just kept on coming.

"She's thirteen," Ella admitted. "About four months pregnant, a prostitute, no prenatal care and she desperately wants to keep the baby."

Her anxiety mounted as the others mumbled their disgust. Thankfully, she managed to keep her attention focused on Roarke, who merely nodded and kept reading.

A moment later, he cocked an eyebrow as he shuffled through yet another report she'd put in the pregnant girl's file. "Her blood looks like it's been whipped through a mixer. Her pregnancy could have thrown her hormones totally out of control. Have you checked for TTP?"

TTP or Thrombotic Thrombocytopenic Purpura. It was a rare condition that she'd only considered when the other lab results had come back clean. TTP could be deadly to both the baby and mother as it turned a pregnant woman's body against her and caused a host of problems from seemingly innocent rashes to awful seizures.

"I'm waiting on those test results now." She wanted to ask him for the required signature right then but, despite her impatience, she figured it was best to wait until he'd read the entire file on the off chance she'd missed something.

Apprehension mounted, and he said nothing as he shifted through more of the contents of the folder.

Ella inhaled slowly, trying to keep a tight grip on her frustration about her young, sick patient. She'd found the pregnant girl huddled on her assigned parking spot in the elaborate Cinder hospital's underground parking lot yesterday morning. How she'd gotten past security, Ella had no idea, but the girl's dark brown eyes had pleaded for her help. She'd said she'd heard of Ella's sympathetic nature and about Cinder's specialized hospital through a mutual friend. Had told Ella she sensed there was something terribly wrong with her pregnancy. Had begged her to save her baby. A moment later, the girl had gone into convulsions right then and there.

"I don't know why you two are even bothering to discuss her case," Manda, snapped as she licked chocolate icing from her fingers. "As you said the slut is homeless and a prostitute. She's scandalous for our hospital. If anyone gets wind of her being here, it could ruin our reputation."

"Her pimp probably holds her purse strings," her other stepsister chimed in. "He won't pay to fix her up. He'll simply get another hooker to take her place."

"She's simply a waste of our time," her stepmother cooed. "Let's please move onto the next case."

The familiar burst of anger erupted inside Ella at their cavalier attitude toward a young woman's life. But she kept her mouth shut and her emotions of disgust and anger well hidden. She'd learned early in life that arguing with her stepfamily was unproductive.

"Let's work like the team we're supposed to be, shall we? Isn't that one of the reasons I was hired for? To shape us all into a team?" Roarke said abruptly. Without waiting for an answer he continued. "This young girl is good promo for Cinder Hospital."

Was that a tinge of anger she detected in his voice? Was it aimed at her? Or the rude, unprofessional behavior of the others?

"How is a homeless, pregnant prostitute good for us?" her stepmother broke in. Her perfectly arched tattooed eyebrows rose in curiosity at Roarke's promo comment.

"We can leak word to the medical press. Tell them that due to the quick thinking of Cinder's hospital staff, a pregnant woman's rare condition was quickly treated and her life was saved. It will give Cinder free promo in the headlines. Other hospitals and doctors will seek us out with their problem pregnancy cases."

"Yeah and those cases won't be able to pay just like this one," Wanda grumbled.

"That's not the point," Roarke said coolly.

Internally Ella cheered him on as he settled casually back against his seat and threw her stepsister a disarming smile. "Our clients will realize we're sympathetic toward the less fortunate. It'll make us appear more...human."

Ouch!

Her stepmother and stepsisters all frowned. It was obvious they didn't like what Roarke was saying. They only took on cases from rich, snobby people who could pay their exorbitant professional fees. Due to the increase in rates, just to subsidize their high living now that her stepfamily had finally drained her father's estate, business for Cinder Gynecological Hospital had taken a downward turn.

"I think what Roarke also means," Ella came to his rescue, taking advantage of the thread he'd created. "We can also leak word to the general public via the newspapers. I know a couple of reporters," she lied. "I can release word we saved the life of a very young pregnant girl. It will garner sympathy in a lot of mothers' eyes. Mothers who have daughters of their own. Mothers who will remember us when their daughters get pregnant and run into medical problems. We'll be discreet about what hits the newspapers. We'll feed them only the appropriate information about a problem case that was quickly solved due to the quick thinking of the Cinder Team. TTP is rare. Most hospitals don't even test for it until they rule out a cause for each symptom as it appears. Those tests can be torturous on the patient. We'll mention we're private. That will eliminate the needy and low-income cases." Of course, she'd forget to mention the private part. As far as she was concerned, she would accept any patient who had a complication in her pregnancy, poor or rich. Payments could be worked out afterwards. "We'll make sure this case hits the medical journals also. As Roarke mentioned, other non-private hospitals will refer their pregnancy problem cases to us especially if they are overcrowded, hence more business for us. I'm sure with Cinder agreeing to pay for the girl's hospital stay and her medication, it's a small cost for all the future business she'll be bringing in."

"Exactly," Roarke slammed the file onto the table and stood. "Now let's get our asses in gear. I don't want to wait for the test results to come in. Let's get her on the meds before it's too late. Ella, she's your client. You tell her what's happening."

"I'll tell her."

"I can see you've already got the requisition form signed. I'll sign it too as your backup and get it over to the nurses' station. They can start administering right away," he said.

Ella nodded, feeling a huge burden lift off her. It felt good having someone else on her side for a change. Very good. However, now wasn't the time to relish in her relief. She had a patient to see.

"Just one moment!" her stepmother snapped as Ella stood. "You stay right there, Ella. Mandy you call an ambulance to get Ella's slut out of here. We cannot go against protocol and administer drugs to someone like that without the proper lab results. We could be sued if Ella is wrong."

"Then they'll have to sue me too," Roarke snapped with irritation.

Ella broke in. "According to Cinder protocol, if two doctors decide it is in the best interest of the patient to administer drugs without having the lab results yet, all that is needed is a second signature. I have that signature from Dr. Stephenson. You wouldn't want to go against our own protocol would you, stepmother?"

Ella didn't wait for her answer. Instead, she forced herself not to smile at the furious looks plastered across her stepmother and stepsisters' faces as she followed Roarke out the door.

.. ∽ ..

LATER THAT DAY ROARKE swore like a son of a bitch when he hopped into his car and maneuvered out of Cinder's parking lot. As the months passed, it became increasingly difficult to remember why he'd taken on this job with the prestigious Cinder Hospital. Lately, he'd had to constantly remind himself that the fantastic pay he received from this establishment would keep his dream alive. A dream he'd been working his ass off for much too long.

Today's case of China had really hit home. Too bad he'd had yesterday off or he would have been able to help the girl earlier. Ella was an excellent doctor. Unfortunately, she'd never had the support she needed from her step-broads and understandably kept her Good Samaritan cases well hidden. This case had been a close call. Too close. If Ella had waited for the test results, the baby and mother could have been irreparably harmed. Or died.

He'd been stunned when he'd found the homeless girl's file sitting right up at the top of today's consultation pile. Either Ella was finally getting herself some balls and standing up for herself and her patients, or she'd just been desperate in this case.

"Fuck!" he slammed his fists against the steering wheel, feeling the gut-wrenching frustration turning his belly into a queasy knot. Why the hell hadn't she called him at home about this case?

Hell! He knew the answer to that. Days off at Cinder were "do not disturb the doctor's day off". No on calls and no midnight surgeries. Just shitty nine-to-five shifts. But that's one of the things that had attracted him to this hospital in the first place. Fantastic pay and evenings free to help take care of his girls.

By day, he gave breast and pelvic exams to rich, horny women who winked and flirted with him as they placed their legs into stirrups and acted as if having a metal probe slip into their vaginas was akin to him fucking them.

Unfortunately, for him, the only pussy he wanted to fuck belonged to sweet, klutzy Ella.

Her shyness and refusal to stand-up for herself irritated him and attracted him at the same time. Overall, she seemed a gentle woman, but on days like today, she proved she had streaks of boldness. To further his irritation, she continued to drown her innocent-looking baby blue eyes behind sexy black-rimmed glasses that simply made his hormones go haywire every time he saw them.

Roarke frowned. Maybe he had a glasses fetish or something? No, it couldn't be that. Every time he saw her, he became transfixed by her compelling beauty. The lack of makeup allowed her skin tone to glow and her natural beauty to shine. Her cheeks always seemed flushed, and although her hair was a mousey blonde and spiky, sometimes windblown, it gave him the impression she'd just tumbled out of bed after a night of mind-blowing sex with some lucky guy.

He'd done some discreet investigating and discovered from the staff as well as some patients, that Ella didn't seem to date and kept mostly to herself.

Too bad he'd decided she was off-limits due to the fact she was a part owner of the hospital. Although she never acted like she was the daughter of the man who'd started the private hospital, he'd decided long ago in his career it was safest to never mix business with pleasure. Or he'd be pursuing Ella with a passion. There was nothing more he wanted than to have her naked and bound. His engorged cock driving shrieks of delight from her flushed body.

Roarke blew out a tense breath. Right now he couldn't think about sexy Ella or he'd end up masturbating right there in the car. He needed to keep his focus on why he'd taken this job and why he'd told everyone at work the big white lie that he had a fiancée.

Truth was, he rarely had the time to date. Speaking of time, he glanced at his watch.

Shit!

If he didn't get home, shower and change, he'd be late for the private adult play of Sinderella showing at his colleague Merck's house. The man was an asshole but he was also an old coworker who knew a lot of important people in the medical profession. Burning bridges with Merck was not an option if he intended to continue climbing up the ladder. Merck was a bit of a ladies' man so he wasn't surprised when the older man had mentioned he was hosting an adult play in his home tonight. Roarke had been invited on several previous occasions but he'd always been busy. Tonight however, he'd decided it was time to cut loose. Merck had also said the play would blow Roarke's mind.

Right then he needed a damn good distraction before his own mind exploded with the anger he felt toward the Cinder bitches casual attitude regarding the less fortunate as well as their mistreatment of Ella. Usually he kept his annoyance well hidden. If he didn't, he'd surely get fired when he told his employers exactly what he thought about their rudeness. The three of them acted so fucking immature that sometimes he simply wanted to tell them to drop-dead or to shove their jobs up where the sun doesn't shine.

But every time he saw Ella he had the totally opposite reaction. He wanted to take her into his arms, kiss her and do so many naughty things to her. Naughty things that would make her blush up a storm.

Today he couldn't help but allow her to see a bit of his soft side, and damned if it hadn't given her a boost. He'd felt quite smug at having her follow him out instead of staying behind as her stepmother had ordered.

Ironic that he was going to see this private Sinderella play. Kind of reminded him of Ella and her mean stepmother and nasty stepsisters.

Gripping the steering wheel tighter, he pressed harder on the gas pedal.

Since before meeting Ella he'd never had any trouble unwinding with some no-holds-barred casual sex with his women friends. Now however, the only person he wanted to have sex with was his klutzy coworker.

Since that was out of the question, he'd just have to force himself to relax tonight. To forget the young, pregnant prostitute who'd reminded him so much of his own young mother and to shove out of his mind the sexy, shy doctor who quite literally had him by the balls.

Chapter Two

ELLA STOOD AT THE BACK door of Merck Manor, a dark brooding castle-like building nestled on seven acres of lush fields in upstate New York. She stifled a sob before shoving yet another tissue beneath the silver mask she wore for her secret performances as Sinderella.

Call her sexually twisted or perhaps she was just shy, but the mask allowed her to participate in many naughty adult scenes.

Sinderella. Her invention. Her naughty secret. Her creative release from reality.

Performing always calmed her down. It was the only time she felt alive and free and separate from her stressful life. Of course keeping her face hidden behind a mask helped. If the people she performed in front of knew her true identity, she'd never be able to do the naughty things she did in front of them. It was because of the luscious sex acts she and her masked troupe performed in the privacy of other people's homes that made Sinderella such a wild success.

If ever there were a night she needed to escape the pressures of her day job, tonight was the night. After seeing China's quick recovery due to the meds Roarke had cosigned, she'd been bawling like a baby. She did that when one of her really sick patients started to get better. She couldn't help being emotional. Had always been that way especially because of her innate ability of putting herself in each of her patient's shoes.

This time the tissue came away damp instead of soaked. Well, at least she was improving.

Running a hand through the shoulder-length, luscious blonde curls of the wig she wore, she looked down at herself and admired the skintight black outfit peeking out from her open spring jacket. The sexy clothing hugged her every sensual curve and allowed a generous amount of skin to show. The halter-top gave quite a revealing view of her creamy breasts and the thong that barely covered her pussy would allow her audience to view her naked ass.

To keep herself in shape for her secret performances, she worked out for a couple of hours every morning in the privacy of her apartment. Aerobics, weight bearing exercises, the treadmill, rowing machine and daily jogging at a nearby park. She did all of it to keep her abs perfectly toned and her body perfectly curvy. Not to mention the exercise helped to wake her up from her naughty, late-night activities.

Excitement began to push away her tears and she rapped on the back door.

She had to wait only a few seconds and the door swung open. Caprice, the motherly woman who Ella had hired to play her fairy godmother in the play, stood there worrying her lower lip.

Uh-oh, when Caprice bit her lower lip it meant trouble. She wasn't wrong.

"Dammit, Sin. Where the hell have you been? The audience is here and they're getting nervous. We were supposed to open fifteen minutes ago," she whispered as she quickly ushered Ella in the back door and down the dimly lit hall of Merck Mansion.

"And Prince Charming never showed either," she added.

"Shit!" Trouble. Big Time.

This just wasn't her day, was it? First she'd had to ask for help with her case and now her freaking Prince Charming had dumped her.

"The next time you hear from him tell him he's fired. We'll start looking for another prince first thing in the morning."

Caprice nodded.

They slid into the room where the rest of the small group had gathered in their colorful, sexy outfits. The instant they saw Ella they stopped talking and waited eagerly for further instructions from her.

God, she loved being the boss. The power made her feel strong and confident—something she never felt in the medical world where her stepsisters and stepmother always managed to make her feel like a clumsy idiot.

"The performance is still on," Ella reassured the small group as she slipped off her jacket and shoes and put on her black dance slippers.

"I've already mentioned to Merck what the problem is, he said he'd be more than happy to play the prince," the petite, white-haired elderly woman who played Prince Charming's mother said innocently.

I'm sure he did.

Merck had a crush on her. Well, maybe a crush was too gentle a word. He wanted her in his bed and that's the last place she ever wanted to be.

"I'll scan the crowd for a prince before any decisions are made." At least that way she'd have some control over what happened tonight. In order for the play to work, she needed someone she was halfway attracted to.

Someone like Roarke.

Just thinking about him made her pussy clench wickedly and cream with liquid heat.

Oh yeah, Roarke would be her perfect Prince Charming. But now was not the time to start fantasizing.

Ella clapped her hands. "Okay everyone. Don't worry. We'll find a prince. As always, let's give them hell tonight!"

The group cheered.

"You guys are the best," Ella complimented her smiling troupe.

She nodded to Caprice who quickly tied the traditional peasant kerchief over Ella's wig and smudged her cheeks lightly with black soot to give the effect of a woman who spent most of her time cleaning.

Then she led Ella from the room. A moment later, she stood outside the door of the room they'd be performing in.

The first act she'd be alone doing a sensual dance while cleaning out the fireplace. She'd also be singing one of the songs she'd learned by heart when she'd been a kid and watched various Cinderella plays over and over again. Of course, she'd made her own adjustments to the tunes, turning it into an adult play her group performed secretly for private audiences. Ella's take of the money went anonymously toward several local charities.

Tonight wasn't the first night she'd have to pick a man from the audience to play her prince. For some reason the part of Prince Charming was the one most often recast...usually because after the show the prince wanted the play to continue...in the bedroom. She had no patience for such unprofessionalism. She considered Sinderella a tasteful, professional, adult spin-off of Cinderella from which, according to the rumors, she'd heard it had been originally invented for adults long before it had been reinvented for children.

Her Sinderella version was a serious, lucrative business and there was no time to play to a man's ego or his aroused cock after the show. It was up to him and not her to get himself relief.

Gosh, she still couldn't believe she did this erotic stuff. If her stepmother and stepsisters found out about her secret life, they'd die right on the spot.

Ella smiled. Wouldn't that be a lovely thing to happen? To see their shocked expressions if they ever discovered their loser, klutzy Ella wasn't as much of a loser or as clumsy as they always teased her about being.

Music drifted from the room. It was her cue.

Swallowing back a last blast of stage fright, she forced herself to glide into the dimly lit room. As she appeared, shocked gasps rang out. A maddening applause quickly followed. The warm welcome washed a sizzling rush through her almost nude body and she couldn't help but be pleased at the way her troupe had decorated the performance room.

Ordinarily Merck used it as his library. On presentation nights, it became Sinderella's living room. Pine beams laced the white stuccoed ceiling and a cheerful fire crackled inside the fieldstone fireplace. Pulled in front of the hearth sat a lone New York ladder-back chair. It would come in very handy in just a few moments.

Grabbing her feather duster with the dildo-shaped handle from the fireplace hearth, she began to dust the furniture and sang her sad tale to the audience of mostly men.

She was Sinderella. Lost in a world of servitude. Her father had married a nasty woman who had two awful daughters. He'd died and her stepfamily had made her their servant. Their slave, who cleaned the chimneys and dusted the house while she fantasized about being rescued from her dismal life.

The song always gripped her heart. It was a song of fantasies. Fantasies of who she wanted to be. Of pretending she was a beautiful princess and had fallen in love with a well-hung prince who would cherish her and make love to her everyday—it made her feel sorry because she knew in reality romance would never happen to her. She was thirty and had never been on a date. Why start now? Sinderella was her sex life and she enjoyed it immensely, even if it wasn't normal behavior for a woman.

While she performed, dancing about with her feather duster, she scanned the excited faces of the numerous male members in her search for a Prince Charming. No one captured her interest tonight.

Frustration began to claw at her belly at the thought of giving in to Merck and allowing him to be her prince. Merck enjoyed tormenting her by dropping hints that if she wanted him to continue to throw private showings for Sinderella, she would have to sleep with him.

He was a millionaire heart surgeon and by far Sinderella's greatest sponsor. She needed to consider his threat and either do as he asked or tell him to shove his request right up his ass.

She leaned heavily to the latter.

Denying Merck would put a dent into the pocketbook of the charities she anonymously donated her share of the Sinderella performances to, but she did have her principles.

Suddenly from the corner of her eye, she noticed a door opening at the other end of the room.

A latecomer.

Her breath caught as she spied the silhouette standing in the open doorway. The play of light and shadow hit his face in just the right way illuminating his profile. Blunt cheekbones, straight nose and sharp angles that made her heart kick-start.

Roarke?

She almost faltered in her song but managed to keep on track, her pulses picking up speed as he hunched into the shadows. He moved with the confidence of a man on the prowl. Just like Roarke.

Oh, no! It couldn't be him, could it?

She noted the extra-wide shoulders, his tall figure. The short haircut and brown hair...

Just like Roarke.

Her body tightened with awareness. Carnal sensations bombarded her most intimate parts. Her nipples elongated. Her breasts wanted to be touched, to be cupped, to be held. Her pussy sizzled to life and ached to be filled by this newcomer's cock.

She almost faltered again as the wicked assault heated her with exquisite want. Almost dropped her feather duster as she slid onto the chair they'd set beside the fireplace just for her.

Angling herself so the newcomer would have the best view, she artfully spread her legs wide, capturing his full attention. Even in the darkness, she felt his hot stare upon her flesh as she teasingly guided the dildo-shaped handle of her feather duster up along her thighs, getting closer and closer to her thong.

She'd known right from the beginning when she'd first conceived the idea for this show that her sexual prowess became heightened when people watched her doing intimate things to herself. Without her face hidden though, she would never have the nerve to be so bold. Would have been much too embarrassed as to what she was doing in front of all these eager patrons.

She continued to sing about her fantasies of a well-hung man coming to her rescue while her free hand tugged at the string holding her thong in place.

The thin garment fell away. Warm air breathed against her pulsing flesh, revealing to all her nude pussy.

Women gasped and men leaned forward in their seats to get a closer look. Sinderella held the newcomer's fierce gaze. .

Using the tip of the dildo, she split her pulsing pussy lips and gently rubbed her engorged clitoris. Within seconds, she felt the familiar stirrings of arousal and couldn't help the moan from escaping her mouth as she dipped inside her entrance, stretching her vagina as she collected the juices quickly accumulating.

Tension mounted inside her as she slid the now lubed dildo over and over her aching clitoris. Her thighs tightened. She forced herself to keep her legs apart, giving the stranger a prelude of things to come should he accept her offer to be her Prince Charming tonight.

Her breaths grew quicker. Her breasts strained against the tight halter.

With her free hand nestled over a clothed breast, she pinched her nipple, gasping at the pleasure-burn.

She continued to rub her sensitive, wet clit. Need grabbed ahold of her pussy. Her body began to ache. Involuntarily her hips arched and gyrated, the fierce arousal rising quickly now.

This act was only one of the erotic sights that made her play famous. She never faked an orgasm during this scene. She knew the tender parts of her body well. Loved touching herself, arousing herself in the privacy of her own bedroom as well as in front of her captive audience. Tonight especially, she enjoyed fucking herself in front of this stranger who looked too familiar.

The newcomer, unlike the other men who leaned forward in their chairs, remained seated in a leisurely, relaxed pose. She sensed he was fully enjoying what she was doing to herself. Could almost imagine his scorching grin. A grin that would look just like Roarke's.

Her breathing stalled. At the thought of this stranger actually being Roarke, the man she'd been fantasizing about for so long, she moved the dildo quicker against her swollen clit, dipping harder into her vagina gathering more of her juices.

Her body sizzled, ached to be touched, to be held by this newcomer. She blew out a breath and almost faltered.

She'd tell Caprice to seek him out when she finished this scene. To ask him if he'd mind being her Prince Charming tonight.

Clenching her teeth, she bit back yet another moan. Her breath halted as the beautiful sensations whipped through her. She shuddered.

Plunging the dildo faster and faster in and out of her pussy, she keened and hissed as the inferno spread. Grinding her hips against the dildo, she finally allowed herself to lose control.

Just before she closed her eyes to welcome her orgasm, she took immense delight when the stranger shifted uneasily in his chair and leaned just a wee bit closer.

Oh yes! Come closer. Come closer.

Ella closed her eyes and groaned out her hot release.

· · ❧ · ·

ROARKE COULDN'T KEEP his eyes off the luscious, curvy blonde. She'd been dancing erotically when he'd arrived, not to mention barely clothed. The carnal sight caught him totally off guard. He'd stood in the doorway transfixed by her beauty. Totally in lust as he'd watched her every movement sensually orchestrated, her voice so soft and familiar it slid over his flesh like a seductive lover's song.

Everything about her called to him. Made his cock shoot into alert mode. Her full, kissable lips reminded him of Ella's. Her long, smooth, feminine legs begged to clasp around his hips. And he found himself wanting to buck his engorged cock in and out of her slit until she cried out in pleasure.

Beneath her skintight halter, he easily made out the two lusciously curved mounds that pushed against the slinky, black lattice cloth. His hands itched to cup her breasts. To feel their weight. His fingers ached to pinch what he could tell were unusually large nipples.

When she'd sat on the chair and spread her legs, her fiery gaze had captured his. He'd been amused at the feather duster turning into a dildo. But when the thong gave way to a deliciously nude pussy, her inner thighs glistening with wetness, her labia plump and her clit red and engorged, Roarke's cock had hardened and lengthened like a thick piece of steel.

His reaction surprised him. Lately he'd only been reacting this violently whenever he got near Ella. From what he could make out about this woman, she did look similar to his klutzy colleague. Maybe that's why he was so captivated with this woman.

He almost laughed at that thought.

Ella and Sinderella were total opposites, but there was something attractive about this woman, just as there was something attractive about Ella.

However, Ella was off-limits. This woman wasn't. He focused his attention on Sinderella.

Every inch of her oozed sexuality. Every soft curve delighted his imagination. Her luscious clit looked engorged and ruby red. Ready for his lips to suck and taste and tease.

His mouth watered at the delicious thought.

She was aroused.

Big Time.

"So? What do you think about Sinderella?" Merck nudged him out of his hot trance. For a moment, Roarke wanted to tell his colleague to fuck off so he could enjoy the show. But it wouldn't do to antagonize Merck. He'd have the information Roarke would need about this mysterious woman.

"Who is she? I'd like to meet her after the show." No use beating around the bush.

"That's the beauty of it. No one knows her true identity. The entire troupe performs with masks and they only accept cash in payment so there's no paper trail. They all leave in separate cars and, from what I've heard, most of the actors don't know her real identity. Maybe you'll get lucky."

Damned right he'd get lucky, Roarke thought as he settled back against his seat to enjoy the show. He couldn't wait to find out more about this mystery woman who hid her face behind that mask. Most of all he needed to find out why she sounded so damned familiar.

• • ⌘ • •

ELLA'S PULSES BLASTED heat through her veins as she awaited her next scene. She'd sent Caprice to do her bidding and wondered if the newcomer sitting in the shadows would accept her offer of being her Prince Charming for the evening. She'd only had to do this on a couple of other occasions and her picks had always been eager, charming and quick learners, yet their cocks had been a little on the small size. For her, size did matter. It just seemed to make the show that much more erotic.

Gosh, she hoped this guy was well-hung.

The rustle of clothing grabbed her attention and Caprice entered the back room where Ella had sequestered herself to mentally prepare for the next scene. It would be her first meeting with the prince.

But who would it be? The sexy newcomer? Or Merck?

"He's agreed."

Yes!

"You've told him everything required of him?"

"He knows what to do. I've got him out back getting into a costume."

Double yes!

"He's quite a hunk. You picked very well, Sin," Caprice complimented as she popped out a compact from nowhere and applied lipstick. "I know he's a lot younger than me, but I think I'm going to have to see if I can't get my hands on him tonight after the performance."

Over my dead body. The thought popped into Ella's head without warning. The intensity of her need to have this stranger all to herself frightened her.

Oh dear. Not good. She couldn't afford to follow these lusty feelings. She needed to keep her mind on the performance, not on the man.

"Sin, ready in five," another performer said as he popped his head inside the room. It was the father of the prince.

She nodded to the man.

Excitement flared as she headed to the door. And to meet her Prince Charming.

Chapter Three

ROARKE SWALLOWED AGAINST the sudden bout of nervousness as he awaited his cue to enter.

He'd been decked out in some unbelievably tight pair of leotard shorts that really enhanced his package.

He'd been stunned when a woman had asked to speak to him privately. She'd whisked him out of the performance room and inquired if he'd mind being Prince Charming to Sinderella.

Hell, he hadn't even thought it over. Had simply reacted and said yes he'd love to. When she'd given him the directions of what would be expected from him during his first scene, it had made his cock hard as stone. So hard, he now ached like a son of a bitch. Yet he wasn't really sure he could go through with this. He'd never acted in front of an audience.

Actually, that wasn't true. He'd done many gyno procedures on sedated women in front of a viewing audience of students. This could be similar...unfortunately, he hadn't been required to take off his clothes, among other things.

Roarke swallowed the tightness in his throat and took a few deep breaths to dispel his nervousness.

Concentrate! Concentrate man!

From the door, he peeked into the room to see what was happening.

At the moment, Sinderella was being chastised by her stepsisters and stepmother for slacking off on her cleaning duties. The pout on her pretty lips slammed into his stomach like a rocket. Those gorgeous lips reminded him so much of Ella. He shook his head at his craziness.

Not possible. Ella would never have the nerve to do what Sinderella had just done. Masturbating in front of a crowd of onlookers took guts. Ella was too shy. Too sweet and innocent.

Most likely she'd be curled up tonight on her couch with her head in a medical book sipping coffee. He found himself chuckling at that thought. Found himself realizing he wouldn't mind cuddling on a couch with her, kissing her ruby-red lips.

Shit! Why did he keep thinking about Ella when he had this luscious woman right in the next room?

"You're not allowed to peek. Come away from there." It was Caprice, her hand curled around his shoulder, and she was pulling at him away from the door.

"Sorry," he muttered. "Just trying to get rid of some of that stage fright."

"Don't worry. Sinderella will be quite pleased with you." Her interested gaze dropped down to parts south. "She picked well."

"She picked?"

Shit! He sounded like an excited schoolboy.

Caprice nodded. "She seemed quite flustered when she asked me to seek you out."

Really? This was damn good news. He'd thought he'd been selected from the audience at random. Now that he knew Sinderella was just as interested in him as he was in her, it made things a little more interesting and a lot more intense.

"Have you memorized what you're supposed to do?"

Roarke nodded. Oh yes, and he'd be surprising Sinderella with a few tricks of his own. By the time he was finished with her, she'd be begging to know his identity and she' be very eager to rip off that sexy silver mask of hers so they could get to know each other a hell of a lot better after the show.

• • ❦ • •

ELLA SWALLOWED AT HER tight throat as the traditional trumpet blew announcing the arrival of the prince. This next scene entailed Sinderella's first meeting with his royal highness...the prince had been to far away lands searching for a wife but had come back empty-handed. Now he was on his way home and had run out of water and was very thirsty.

As he entered the room, his face concealed by a sparkling blue mask, Ella's pulses began to pound in wicked anticipation.

Wow! He was built! He wore nothing but skintight shorts that perfectly outlined his huge cock and swollen balls.

Ella licked her lips. Very nice! Very nice, indeed.

"Hello! My lovely wench." The prince said as he neared her. His deep, masculine voice sent shock waves coursing up her spine.

It had to be Roarke!

Hot eyes peered back at her through the slits in the mask. Excitement flared and her body heated with fierce awareness as he read the handful of lines Caprice had given him to remember.

"I'm very thirsty," he said. "May I draw some water from your well?"

Oh dear! If this was Roarke...

"I'm sorry, my Prince, but the well is dry."

She could hear his breath quicken. Did he recognize her voice? She'd changed the tone and depth, but did he know? Her throat grew dry as he drew closer. Anxiety snapped through her, as she awaited his next words.

His gaze locked with hers. Although she could barely see his eyes in the darkness of the mask, the sensuality of his look seared into her like a rocket. So intimate she almost forgot about the audience watching them.

"Then you wouldn't mind if I quench my thirst upon your lusty body?"

"I...I don't know. I should seek permission from my family, but they are not at home," she replied.

"I'm too thirsty to wait. Would you have my death upon your head?"

"No, I could not. I must submit to you, my Prince."

Readying herself to sit on the chair, she gasped as his hands seared into the naked flesh of her waist. Masculine heat hugged her as he pulled her into a tight embrace.

What the hell? This wasn't part of the performance.

"First a kiss from your sweet lips for a parched man," he said softly.

Oh no, a kiss was not in the play.

She could feel the coiled tension in his body. The soft press of his chest against her breasts. The rock-hard cock branding her lower belly.

Her pussy quivered, whether out of fear of his massive size or out of excitement, she wasn't sure. He gripped her waist tighter, as if sensing her confusion.

Then his head was lowering and the breath in her lungs stalled.

For a moment, she thought of turning her head away. Of regaining some measure of control, but the instant his warm, firm lips touched hers; she became lost in a swirl of lusty tensions.

She could barely think as his tongue speared into her mouth.

Possession.

Desperation.

Desire.

Eagerness. She sensed it all in his heated kiss.

His mouth burned into hers as he explored. His tongue smoothed over her teeth, mated with her tongue. The brand of his hands slid down her body, cupping her naked ass cheeks. The push of his thick bulge against her lower belly grew harder. The intimate gesture made her vagina clench with primal demand. She melted against his hard contours and boldly pressed her pussy against his erection.

He groaned. It was a sensual sound. One like she'd never heard before.

She shivered. Fire raged through her veins. She could barely draw in a breath when he abruptly broke the intoxicating kiss.

She couldn't resist him as he led her to the chair by the fireplace and made her sit. She watched as he got down on one knee between her widespread legs. The wicked burn of his fingers over her knees had her grabbing the edge of the chair just to keep herself steady.

With a quick tug, her thong left her body.

"I'm so thirsty...you will not deny me a drink from your well." His voice sounded strangled, aroused.

How could she resist? She couldn't even speak. Couldn't move. Her body felt so tight with anticipation. Her breaths came in such harsh gasps.

"Your pussy is as red as wine," he said, the tip of his tongue peeked out from his luscious mouth. The sight mesmerized her. Sent her pulses careening.

He leaned his head between her thighs, his hot breath blazing against her pussy.

"Oh, my God," she found herself whispering, her performance lines totally forgotten as she noted his familiar silhouette.

It had to be Roarke!

She could never have imagined in any of her fantasies, the anticipation, the sweet torture gathering inside her at the sight of Roarke going down on her. Since he was a newcomer without experience in acting, Caprice had instructed him to simply place his mouth over her pussy, allowing her to fake the orgasm. But the strong, moist tongue that licked between her pulsing labia made her just about come out of her chair. She couldn't help but cry out at the fire of his touch and the erotic bristle of his stubble rasping against her tender flesh.

Sweet mercy! Roarke certainly knew how to orally pleasure a woman.

For the first time in her life, she allowed herself to simply feel.

It felt damn good as he sucked a plump labia into his mouth. The heat of his lips branded her. His teeth nibbled gently on her flesh. Fire raged. He seduced her other labia in the same way. Then slid his tongue over and over her clit until her fists turned into tight knots and her lower belly clenched erotically.

When his tongue dove into her slit, she simply came apart. Blades of pleasure zipped through her and she barely heard the strangled cry ripped from her throat as Roarke's tongue plunged in and out of her like a miniature cock. Shudders ran rampant.

Tossing her head back, her lips parted to allow her pants to escape.

His tongue continued the erotic thrust. His nose acted like a clit stimulator, pressing, smoothing, until pleasure spiraled and her cream gushed down her channel.

Slurps quickly followed as he drank greedily from her.

Erotic sensations continued to tear through her, and when he finished, she felt weak from the climax.

"Thank you for quenching my thirst, oh beautiful wench."

Her pussy still fluttered in the glorious aftermath and she found it hard to open her eyes at the sound of his voice. When she did, he was licking her come off his lips. His chin and nose shone with her juices.

He remained on one knee and she trembled in awe at the way his chest muscles rippled as he released her legs.

"You taste so sweet, like wine. What is your name, lass?"

The soft caress of his words almost had her telling him her real name. She caught herself at the last moment.

"Sinderella, my Prince."

"Sinder...ella." Her name rolled off his tongue in two syllables. The Ella part more pronounced.

Her pulses faltered in a sudden bout of fear. Did he know her true identity? But how could he? She always borrowed a friend's car to come to the performances so no one could trace her. Always removed any jewelry from her body that would give her identity away. Unless he'd recognized her voice? Surely if he had, he would have said something.

No, she was just clasping at straws. He had no idea who she really was.

He stood.

"Alas, my thirst has been quenched as it has never been quenched before. I shall never forget your hospitality or you."

He bowed and then he was gone. Leaving her staring after him. Wanting him. Needing him.

The audience clapped. It was a roar unlike any she'd ever heard before and it sent tingles of happiness slithering up her spine. Obviously, they'd enjoyed the performance just as much as she'd enjoyed what Roarke had done to her. The applause faded.

She trembled when she heard the laughter of her approaching stepfamily. It was her cue to continue straight into the next scene. A small scene with her two stepsisters and evil stepmother complaining how tired they were after a day of shopping.

It took every ounce to gather her wits to continue on track with the play. She'd never found it so difficult to concentrate on her lines. Fire laced her pussy. Sticky dampness clung to her inner thighs as she quickly retrieved her thong and tied it back into place.

She wanted to go after Roarke. Wanted to grab him. Push him up against the wall and just fuck him. She blew out a tense breath.

Wow! She'd never had such a fierce urge to be fucked. To fuck.

She wanted more of those delicious licks he'd given her. At the same time, her mind whirled in disbelief.

Had she really been mouth-fucked by Roarke? Or had she just fantasized it was him and actually given his face to the newcomer?

Passion pounded through her as she suddenly remembered the other delights in store compliments of her Prince Charming.

• • ❧ • •

"FUCK! YOU LUCKY DOG, Roarke. I've been trying forever to get inside her pussy. How did the bitch taste?" Merck was laughing and slapping congratulations on Roarke's back as Roarke changed into yet another pair of skintight attire. This time he would wear nothing but a thong.

Being practically naked in front of people who knew him made him a bit nervous, but Merck's crude comment about Sinderella sliced deep into his gut and he resisted the urge to take a swing at the man.

"You'll never know, will you?" Roarke growled.

Merck backed up a step, obviously picking up on his hostility. "Take it easy, man. She's just a slut."

Roarke saw red.

Before he knew what happened, he'd grabbed Merck by his shirt collar and pushed him up against a nearby wall. The sharp sound of a whoosh as the wind left Merck's lungs and the way he blinked back at him—totally stunned—made Roarke regain his senses. However the red-hot anger remained.

"You're a fucking asshole," Roarke hissed, and let go of Merck. "She's not a slut. She's an actress doing her job."

"And it seems her pussy cream has drugged you, my friend." Merck chuckled as he straightened his tie. "Maybe I'll have to get myself a little taste too."

Before he could tell Merck to back off, the bastard had already slipped away.

Clutching his hands into fists, Roarke fought the anger. He was being ridiculous. The woman in the play was just an actress. She was used to having a man's mouth on her pussy. It was part of the act. Caprice had instructed him that because he wasn't trained, he would only have to place his mouth over Sinderella's pussy and she would fake the rest. However, when he'd gotten between her legs, he'd been enticed by her overpowering scent of arousal. He'd simply had to taste her, pleasure her, fuck her with his tongue.

Roarke closed his eyes and stifled a moan. She'd tasted so fine. Addictive like a fruity, expensive ice wine. The intense way her vaginal muscles had eagerly clenched around his tongue...well, he knew she'd been pleased with the oral sex he'd given to her.

No faking orgasms tonight, Sinderella. Not if he continued to get his way, which by the way her shoulders had tensed up as he'd leaned closer to kiss her, led him to believe she wasn't used to not being in control where the play was concerned.

When he'd pulled her against him, he'd sensed her fear, her indecision.

She'd fit perfectly against him. Soft flesh in all the right places. Her curves melting against his hard planes. She was even the same height as Ella.

Not to mention how innocently she'd kissed. As if she were inexperienced.

Roarke's eyes snapped open at the thought.

Jesus.

Could Sinderella be more innocent than she let on?

•• ❧ ••

"HERE'S THE NEW DRESS for the Prince's Ball as promised," Caprice cooed proudly as she entered the back room where Ella had sequestered herself, the harsh, crinkling sound of plastic following her inside. "And before I present it to you, I have to say you did a fabulous performance with the prince. He really brought out the best acting in your career. You really looked like you were climaxing." She wiggled her eyebrows and laid the unwrapped dress on a nearby chair.

"I was climaxing," Ella admitted, still trying to settle her nerves over what had just taken place with Roarke and what would be coming during her next meeting with him.

Caprice's mouth opened in shock. "No way, are you serious?"

Ella nodded.

"Oh, my God! I specifically told him what to do, and going down on you was not in my instructions."

"Obviously he has problems following the rules."

"Obviously. And what was with the kiss? You've never allowed a prince to kiss you before...at least not until the last scene."

"I couldn't stop him." Hadn't really wanted to.

"Like hell. Did you ever hear of slapping his face?" Caprice snapped. "I cannot believe he would take advantage of you like that in front of an audience. I've always told you I do not like it when you pick right from an audience. It's too risky. We should have cancelled tonight's performance. I'm going to have a chat with that man and tell him we've got rules." Caprice started for the door.

"No, don't. I've got my own revenge plans for him."

"Ella. We're professionals. We've got a pristine reputation. We can't afford to screw it with games."

Ella smiled. "Don't worry, Mom," she said using Caprice's nickname affectionately given to her by the troupe. "I'll stay on track with the show. There won't be any surprises." Except for Roarke. A surprise he'll truly enjoy.

"Now get rid of your frown and let's take a look at that sexy new dress you made for me."

. . ❧ . .

"JUST REMEMBER, MY SWEET Sinderella, miracles are happening everyday. All you have to do is believe in the magic. Believe in the magic of miracles and a miracle will come true for you," her fairy godmother cooed as she and Ella stood in the middle of Sinderella's living room. Her stepsisters and stepmother had already left for the Prince's Ball, leaving Sinderella crying and desolate that she was prohibited to go because she had her cleaning duties to attend to.

She'd wanted so badly to see the prince again. Wanted so badly to have his mouth on her pussy again.

"But I do believe in the magic of miracles, Fairy Godmother," she said, following the lines of the play.

Sweet mercy! She really did believe in miracles tonight. Especially now that she'd had the pleasure of kissing the man of her fantasies. Of having his head between her thighs, licking and sucking on her pussy, making her experience the best orgasm she'd ever had in her life.

"Then close your eyes, Sinderella. Close your eyes and believe in the magic of miracles."

"But I cannot attend the Ball wearing these rags, Fairy Godmother. I need a beautiful gown."

"Believe it and it will happen."

She closed her eyes and knew the cinematic smoke would gush through the performance room.

"Hurry, hurry," Caprice said. Ella's eyes popped open, and it took only a quick tug on her halter and thong and she stood naked in the smoke. Lifting her arms, she allowed Caprice to slide the slinky dress over her. It fit like a glove.

Personally, she'd always wished for a fairy godmother. Someone sweet and nurturing like her motherly friend who would help her garnish her self-esteem and self-confidence. Someone who would grant her wishes and make all her dreams come true, someone who would banish her insecurities around men she felt sexually attracted to...men like Roarke.

She'd never had sex with a man without her mask. In a way, she was a relationship virgin. Always avoiding men because she didn't really know how to act around them. Didn't possess the self-confidence or self-esteem to be bold enough to go after Roarke, no matter how much she craved to.

She knew she shouldn't, but she'd always blamed her father for her troubles. For him being such a damn fool in picking the wrong woman for himself and for her, thus ruining her childhood. She'd been only five when her beautiful mom had died in childbirth. Her baby sister had died a day after, leaving Ella without a mother or a sibling. Her father became so obsessed with his private hospital that she rarely saw him anymore. At that point, her craving for his attention grew and her interest in becoming a gynecologist just as he was took root.

She still remembered the amused way her father had laughed at her when she'd told him in her naïve five-year-old, defiant stance that she wanted to skip school for the rest of her life so she could go to work with him and learn everything about his doctoring trade.

His laughter at her newfound dream had stung. Had ripped a hole in her soul. He'd merely patted her on the head like she was an amusing dog and ushered her off to school with the nanny he'd hired. A year later, he'd married a gynecologist who worked at the hospital, saddling Ella with two stepsisters. They were horrid creatures, already in their early teens. They ignored her and studied hard so they could go to medical school and be doctors themselves. They garnered all the attention from her father and new stepmother, leaving her totally alone and frustrated.

In turn, Ella threw herself into her fantasy world. Studying ballet, taking singing lessons and doing anything that would keep her mind occupied at her growing insecurities that she would never be the doctor she wanted to be.

One year later her father died of a massive heart attack, leaving her an unloved stepchild who was shipped off to an all-girls private school so fast it had literally made her head spin. Over the years in the school, she'd continued her dance lessons, singing lessons and even taken acting classes.

When she graduated, her stepmother presented her with the trust fund her father had set up with the provision Ella study gynecology and become a doctor so she could carry on with the rest of the family in the family business.

In the end, she had succeeded in what she'd wanted to do with her life. She had become a doctor. Unfortunately all her studying and seclusion in her fantasy world hadn't prepared her for interacting with the opposite sex. Hence her creation of Sinderella, which enabled her to hide behind a mask as she dabbled in sex with strange men. Men who seemed to fall in love with the fictional Sinderella, but not really with her. Well, maybe if she'd given them the chance they would have loved her, but she'd been unable to remove her mask to get intimate with them.

"And now, sweet, sexy Sinderella, you will go to the Ball," her fairy godmother's voice made her snap from her thoughts. "Just remember you must leave the Ball before midnight for then the beautiful, sexy clothing will vanish and you will return to the rags you had before."

The audience clapped their appreciation as Sinderella was ushered from the room to await the next scene with her prince.

. . ❧ . .

ROARKE BLEW OUT A TIGHT breath as he heard the audience clapping and whistling in appreciation.

Shit! They really seemed to be enjoying themselves.

He wished he could be out there in the audience seeing what that sexy woman was up to. But he'd only be squirming impatiently in his chair. Craving her, needing to be inside her, wanting to know exactly what kind of a woman would be bold enough to masturbate in front of a live audience as well as allow a complete stranger to go down on her with thirty or so people watching them.

His cock pulsed violently against his thong and he almost groaned aloud at what would transpire between them at the Ball.

"It's time," Caprice said as she and the rest of the troupe, all decked out in sexy, sultry party clothes, moved like one well-oiled machine toward the door.

He was impressed he had to admit as he followed them out into the hallway straining his neck in order to catch a glimpse of his sultry, sexy Sinderella.

To his disappointment, she was nowhere to be found. A sliver of frustration nibbled at him. It made him wonder if the real Prince Charming had felt this same kind of frustration when he'd gone about town placing glass slippers on women's feet, hoping to find the woman who had eluded him at the Ball.

Oh shit, get this crap out of your brain, man. It's just fantasy.

Short of ripping the mask from her face, he might never find out the woman's identity. At least that's what he'd learned from the group of actors who, after working with her for a couple of years, still didn't know the identity of their boss. They'd also explained about what had happened to the other princes who'd fallen for the elusive Sinderella. One by one they'd become frustrated with not being able to find out who she was and had quit.

He wouldn't quit that easily.

Before the night was out, he would have her silver mask in his hands or, at the very least, have a way of finding out her true identity. Of that, he was certain. No sane man would put up with what had transpired between the two of them in front of the audience tonight and not want more from her.

Chapter Four

ELLA TWISTED HER FINGERS into anxious knots as she waited outside the door to where the play was taking place. Cripes! She wanted so badly to get a look at her prince. Wanted to push open the door. To run inside and tell him she was Ella. That she wanted him to fall in love with her and not with Sinderella.

Caprice seemed to sense her need and kept her figure smack-dab in her way, preventing her from so much as taking a peek through the doorway at the prince who by then must have danced with Sinderella's two evil sisters. One anorexic. The other extremely overweight.

When Sinderella had been looking to hire the sisters, she'd made sure they reminded her of her own stepsisters. It gave her a morbid satisfaction during the performances when she ended up with the prince and not them. Perhaps this was her immature way of acting out against her own stepfamily.

Whatever the reason, she'd never been so nervous about performing in her life as she was tonight. Come to think of it, ever since she'd caught sight of Roarke's shadowy figure tonight she'd been on the sexual edge of hell.

"I've been told your prince is just as eager to get together again with you as you are with him."

Oh dear. Now she was even more nervous.

Mom smiled softly. "Do you by any chance know him?"

"Good God! Why in the world would you ask that?"

"Because I've never seen you like this before. Your cheeks are so flushed and you're trembling. Not to mention the way you seduced that dildo duster and kept your eyes glued in his direction when you orgasmed—it was as if you were making love to him and not the audience. You should know that's a no-no, Sin. Work the audience. That's always been our number-one rule."

"Sorry, I'll do better." God! She couldn't believe she was actually apologizing to her employee.

"Sweetheart, I know you will. I just thought I should mention it."

"I'm glad you did, Mom."

She needed to concentrate. Needed to make this a fantastic performance. Merck was a very rich man and he had deep pockets. The friends he brought here also had deep pockets. They paid handsomely to see the private production.

The sound of a trumpet announcing her arrival snapped her to reality. It was her cue to enter.

For a split second, she hesitated.

Dare she go in there? She could screw this up because of her nervousness performing with Roarke.

"Go, go, go," Mom whispered.

Ella nodded and took a deep breath. Renewed gasps of approval zipped through the air as she entered the room dressed in the beautiful, sultry, skintight dress. Of course while she'd been out of sight, there had been a couple of surprises added, but her audience and Roarke would discover it soon enough.

The loudest gasp came from Prince Charming who stood in the corner in front of the king and queen, his parents.

The intense way he watched her made her breath ram right up into her lungs. If looks could undress her, then this man was doing it.

For the first time since she'd started Sinderella, she wanted her mask to be smaller...to be gone.

His mask gone.

As she approached Roarke, he stood there and stared at her. His intense gaze caressed her skin. Made her feel hot all over.

She wore the sexiest, clingiest, tightest white spandex mid-hip-length dress. The material shimmered with the wet look and hugged her every curve to perfection. The front had an adjustable lace-up cord that revealed her belly button and could reveal as little or as much of her breasts as she wanted.

In anticipation of tonight, she'd left the strings so loose that her prince would have little trouble at getting easy access to her.

She shivered beneath his hot stare and the room grew deathly quiet as he moved toward her. His steps were long, confident. It made her heart race with excitement.

His cock seemed so much bigger now. The swollen outline nestled between two perfectly shaped spheres fired her blood. Velvety muscles laced his chest and he wore a white mask.

He was a devastatingly handsome man. A man she wanted in her bed with his hard, long cock plunging in and out of her in uncontrollable thrusts.

At those thoughts, her breaths came faster, harder. His breathing grew louder, raspier, as he held out his hand. Such a wonderfully large hand. A hand meant for caressing her skin, for touching her breasts and a whole bunch of naughty things.

"Shall we dance?" he asked in a low voice that melted over her.

She nodded. Placing her fingers against his warm palm, she immediately sensed the erotic tingles of awareness zip through her. He pulled her close, pressed his body intimately against hers. Pushed that wonderful bulge tightly against her lower abdomen.

Her pussy reacted immediately. Grew hot and wet. Her vaginal muscles clamped around empty air.

She moaning aloud.

Oh, goodness!

"Have we by chance met before? You seem familiar to me, my Princess," he asked, saying the lines that were expected from him. She sensed he wasn't acting. He was serious.

"Anything is possible, my Prince," she replied.

He smiled and she noticed immediately he wasn't the best of dancers when he stepped on her toes.

Music filtered through the room. They danced to a slow waltz, gazing into each other's eyes as if there weren't thirty people watching them.

For Ella, they were alone.

He moved against her in a sensual rhythm. One hand at her waist, his fingers branding through her clothing. His other hand remained intimately intertwined with her fingers.

His cock burned against her, making her blood pump strong and fast. She answered his rhythm by softly grinding against him, slowly swaying her hips. He inhaled sharply. She noticed his jaw clenched.

Her mind reeled with happiness. He was just as turned-on as she was.

They remained silent as they danced, but she could feel his hot gaze beaming through the mask, burrowing into her skin like a blast from a furnace. When the music finally came to an end, she was breathing so hard and so fast in anticipation of what would come next, she actually felt a bit faint.

"Who are you?" he whispered the words so softly she wasn't even sure he'd said them.

Suddenly his head lowered. She trembled and held her breath, thinking he was going to kiss her, instead his warm lips nibbled along the side column of her neck midway between her ear and her shoulder. The erotic touches sent ripples of shivers tingling up her back making her body tighten with exquisite need, and she couldn't stop the soft whimper that escaped her mouth.

He stayed there at her neck, his demanding lips nibbling at her tender flesh. Sucking gently at first, then harder until a sweet burst of pain from his sharp teeth made her whimper again. He calmed the fire he'd created with long, wet strokes of his tongue until her flesh throbbed wonderfully before he pulled slowly away.

The area that he'd bitten, throbbed.

Then he spoke, his voice a low, tortured whisper so only the two of them could hear. "I would make love to you right here and now, up against the wall, but I want our first time to be alone."

Her body tightened against his words.

The lights dimmed setting the next scene.

"You're a very beautiful woman. Very desirable. I find you quite irresistible, my Princess," Prince Charming said louder this time so the audience could hear.

"And I you," she replied, her heart now beating against her chest like a battering ram.

Oh boy, did she ever want him!

She trembled as he reached for the string holding her corset dress in place. It only took one pull and the strings loosened, allowing him to slide the material over her shoulders, allowing her breasts to spill free in front of him.

And in front of the audience.

She heard the soft inhalations from some of the men. The excited whispers of women when they noticed she wore nipple rings with thumb-sized sparkling glass slippers attached.

Prince Charming was breathing hard. His Adam's apple moved wildly as he swallowed.

"Exquisite breasts," he said hoarsely.

She'd had her nipples pierced a couple of years ago. It allowed her to dress her breasts in some unique ways for her show. By the way Roarke sounded, he certainly appreciated how she'd decorated herself.

He licked his lips and Ella followed the movement of his rosy tongue. Sexual hunger roared through her. She'd never been turned-on so hot and so fast by the sight of a man's tongue.

She held her breath as his head lowered toward her right breast.

She moaned aloud at the whispering impact of his wet tongue teasing the tip of her pierced nipple. Gasped as he placed his lips over her entire pink nipple, including the ring with the dangling glass slipper.

He sucked. Hard.

Lightning streaks seared a line from her breast straight into her pussy.

More! She wanted more!

Automatically her legs parted. Oh boy, did she ever want his mouth down there too.

Her urgency made her moan. Made her want him to rebel against the storyline and simply take her pussy with his cock.

Sharp teeth nipped at the tip of her aching nipple. Pleasure-pain sliced through her breast. Sensitive nerve endings shimmered as his fingers cupped her other breast, squeezing, kneading, massaging, making her flesh swell with arousal.

At the same time, he continued to savage her nipple. His fierce licks, sharp nips and long pulls made her moan louder.

When he had finished tending both her breasts, she felt drugged with pleasure-pain. It left her so hot and achy she just wanted his cock buried deep inside her. Even with all these people watching.

Then his earlier words whispered at the back of her mind.

I want our first time to be alone.

She didn't think she could wait that long.

When he drew away, she reached out to him. She wanted to touch him. To make sure he was real. Make sure he was actually Roarke and not just wishful thinking or another fantasy.

Her fingers hungrily explored the raspy stubble on his cheeks and chin. The smooth curvature of his moist lips. The strong, corded column of his neck.

Her hands splayed over his velvety chest muscles. When her fingernails scraped the tips of his nipples, she heard him groan in response.

Ella smiled.

Payback is a bitch, Roarke. But a very nice bitch. Now it was her turn to get even.

Ella's hands trailed over his hot, tight abdomen. Hard muscles quivered beneath her fingertips. Quivered with anticipation. With need.

She slipped downward to his waist, to where the white thong held his erection hostage. She pulled the material and it fell away.

She gasped in surprise at the immense size of his erection. Heard the females in the audience gasp in appreciation. Some of the men swore softly, enviously.

Fierce need consumed her at the juicy sight. Roarke was naked. Powerfully naked.

Nestled amidst a spattering of dark, curly hair, surrounded by a couple of perfectly shaped, swollen testicles, his cock looked stone-hard and curved upward against his abdomen.

Her pussy contracted wickedly. He must be at least ten inches long, maybe even three inches thick.

Prime male. Her fantasy man come to life.

Only better.

"Do I please you, my Princess?"

She nodded, her lines totally forgotten. She couldn't take her gaze from the spectacular sight. Roarke was bigger than she'd ever imagined.

She licked her lips. Felt her naked breasts swell, ache. Her pussy creamed. She could feel the warm stickiness flowing down along her inner thighs.

"I take it my princess is at a loss for words."

The audience chuckled, broke her trance.

"Oh yes, my Prince. Oh yes, your size does please me!"

"I've never felt this way about a woman before."

"And I have never felt this way about a man."

"You have made me so horny, my beauty. Pleasure me, my Princess."

He stroked his straining arousal, and his cock twitched like a live wire.

Ella shuddered with longing. Her body hungered for him. She wanted his huge cock buried deep inside of her.

"I will pleasure you, my Prince. I will show you that I am worthy of your intentions."

He made a move to retrieve one of the flavored condoms kept on a nearby chair for such occasions, but she grabbed his wrist, stopping him.

"No, my Prince."

She heard the soft whispers signal uneasiness through the audience.

Perhaps they thought she would deny the prince, or perhaps they were shocked at her break in protocol. Sinderella always practiced safe oral sex with the prince wearing a condom, but this time...this time it was Roarke. This time she would make an exception.

"I want no barriers between us tonight, my Prince," she said loud enough for the audience to hear.

His lips tightened. Was it in arousal? Or in disapproval.

"I will trust you. If you will trust me," she whispered softly so only the two of them could hear.

"I'm clean," he whispered back. "And I trust you."

Warmth spread through her at his words and she smiled. Dropping to her knees in front of him, she eagerly opened her mouth and he guided his swollen cockhead toward her face. She wrapped one hand around the pulsing base, his flesh felt like lightning-hot, silk-encased steel against her fingers and palm.

Looking up, she saw the controlled set of his jaws, but he couldn't hide the rapid rise and fall of his naked chest. His hard flesh slid between her lips and her tongue immediately dove against the tiny slit in his bulging head. She tasted the salty pre-come of his arousal. Swirled her tongue around his impressive flesh, savoring his masculine heat, feeling the pulsing veins straining against his rigid cock.

With her other hand she gripped his firm hip, steadying herself. She could hear his harsh breaths split the air. Felt the carefully restrained thrust of his hips as he moved against her. She began to suck his cock. Her mouth was a tight suction as he slid in and out, going deeper with his every delicious thrust. She moved her hand farther up the hard shaft to the point where she could safely take some of his length.

Rubbing her tongue along the sensitive bottom of his cock, she took great pleasure in hearing his groans. The erotic sounds sifted through her, warming her pussy, making her cream over and over.

Taking her time with Roarke, she teased his shaft by gently biting down, allowing her teeth to scrape along his tender flesh as he plunged in and out of her mouth.

His groans grew louder, wilder.

His hands speared through her wig, holding her head captive. His fingers tightened against her scalp and she knew he was dangerously close to losing control.

She backed off, relishing his moans of protest.

Oh yes, she had Roarke right where she wanted him—at her mercy.

Her tongue cradled his cock, welcomed him in. But her teeth, ah yes...her teeth were just about bringing him to his knees. His cock jerked and pulsed in what she perceived as him experiencing pleasure-pain.

Again, she increased the pressure of her teeth against the frantic plunges. Enjoyed the untamed groans.

She loved the feel of his cock sliding in and out of her mouth. The velvety skin. The rock-hard flesh. The powerful taste of man and musk.

She sucked harder. He thrust his hips harder.

"I'm coming," he suddenly gasped.

In the past, the prince would spew into his condom and then throw it into the nearby flickering fireplace. With the change in protocol, Roarke probably felt unsure of what to do.

Digging fingers harder into his hip, she pulled him closer. If that didn't give him an indication of what she wanted, she then tightened her lips around his shaft and she sucked with all her might.

"Oh, yes!" he ground out as his thrusts came quicker. His cock grew tense. Jerked.

Then she savored what she'd worked so hard to get. Loved the thick jets of his warm semen as he came inside her mouth.

Ella swallowed every drop.

When he was spent, he slumped onto the nearby chair. Crystal beads of perspiration dampened his chest. His eyes were scrunched tightly. His lips parted from his harsh gasps.

Ella smiled despite the arousal roaring through her.

Sitting down wasn't a part of the show, but in this case he'd be excused.

"Did I please you, my Prince?" Her voice shook and his eyes blinked open. A knowing grin flittered across his delicious mouth.

"I have fallen in love with you, my Princess."

"And I with you, my Prince."

The clang of the clock striking midnight made Ella groan her frustration.

Oh, God! Not now. The sound was her cue to run from the Ball.

"I must leave," she said, and she stood.

"But you've only just gotten here, my love."

My love. That wasn't part of the script.

In the background, the strike of the midnight bell continued to clang.

Oh damn! She didn't want to leave. She wanted to stay there with Roarke. Enjoy more of this fantasy play.

Unfortunately, if she didn't go at the strike of midnight, it would ruin the show. She had an audience watching them. An audience she'd totally forgotten in her haste to have Roarke's delicious cock.

Ella headed for the door. Her legs felt weak, her pussy sopping wet and, to her horror, she almost forgot to drop the nipple ring with the glass slipper onto the floor.

· · ∾ · ·

"WHAT IN THE WORLD HAPPENED out there? Are you insane? We always practice safe sex! I can't believe what you've done!" Caprice hissed as she and a couple of the troupe ushered her to the nearby dressing room.

"Slight deviation from the plan," she answered truthfully. But she wanted more of the deviation. She could feel the sticky wetness of her arousal. Could feel her engorged clit throbbing in desire, her pussy aching to be fulfilled.

A roar of applause, whistles and shouts followed.

"That's the scene ending. He must have found the nipple ring. Why did you do the oral sex without a condom? God, please tell me you had a good reason, sweetheart. Please tell me you haven't lost your mind?"

"Mom, rest assured I do know what I am doing. Please trust me," Ella reassured the frantic woman.

"Okay, okay. I trust you. I do. I really do. I know you do things for a reason."

"Did the audience seem to be okay with it?" She'd been so greedy in not thinking about their reaction. Most of them were from the medical profession. Doctors, nurses and others she'd seen at medical conferences. They would not be pleased.

"I hadn't realized. I was too busy watching the two of you."

Shoot!

"Okay. Spread it around that we know each other. That we trust each other." Her admission of the truth was her only source of damage control. Her only way to show she had been a responsible adult tonight. She truly did trust Roarke. Instincts told her he would never put her in any kind of danger, sexual or otherwise.

"I knew it! You two have a sexual energy that permeates the room. You looked absolutely smashing together and you act so naturally with each other," Caprice cooed. "You obviously enjoyed him. We should hire him."

"No. He can't be my prince."

"Surely we can—"

"I said no!" Ella found herself snapping as reality reared its ugly head. She couldn't chance Roarke finding out about her secret life. He could not know she was Sinderella. If he found out, then her life would be too distracting at work. Hell, with her frequent fantasies about him, it was already too distracting at work. Surely with tonight's experience popping into her mind whenever she saw him, her klutziness around him was bound to worsen?

Oh, God! What was she going to do?

She caught Caprice frowning at her.

"I'm sorry for snapping at you, Caprice. I didn't mean to. It's just he can't know who I am."

"Well, you're the boss, sweetie," her fairy godmother said calmly, embracing Ella in a hug she really needed. "You've never steered us wrong before. If you don't want him for your Prince Charming, I'll tell the rest of the troupe before they get too excited. I'll drop word to the audience you are intimately involved and trust each other."

"Okay," Ella nodded.

Caprice let her go and smiled warmly, knowingly. "Are you sure you don't want him?"

"I'm sure." *Liar!*

"Okay, get yourself ready for the next scene."

With a soft rustle of clothing, Caprice left the dressing room.

But I want him to be my prince. I want him to be mine. All mine.

Closing her eyes, she concentrated really hard and whispered to herself. "I believe in the magic of miracles. I truly believe. Roarke will some day become my Prince Charming in every way."

·· ✿ ··

ROARKE WAS STILL SAVORING the sweet, erotic way Sinderella's tight little mouth had wrapped so perfectly around his penis when a sharp rap at the door cued him to get his ass in gear for the final scene.

He'd never seen a more erotic sight than having that gorgeous woman drop down on her knees in front of him. He'd been told what would transpire. Had been told to ejaculate into a condom and throw it into the fireplace, but when he'd tried to follow the rules, Sinderella had turned the tables on him.

No condom. Her grip had tightened. The sensual way her mouth had worked his cock made him her prisoner. At her mercy.

He'd never known a woman to go down on him so eagerly. So unconditionally. Sweet, sexy Sinderella. The woman of his dreams. His woman in every way.

Or she would be...when the time was right.

Chapter Five

"I HAVE FOUND YOU. I have found the love of my life," he said.

Ella held her breath as nude from the waist up, Roarke's warm, slightly trembling fingers brushed against her naked breast as he quickly inserted the missing nipple ring with the sparkling glass slipper.

"We will be together. Forever," he said softly, and she accepted the prince's warm hand. His fingers clasped intimately with hers and he squeezed gently when they both bowed, indicating the performance was completed.

The applause was deafening. The audience stood and Sinderella held her breath at the sight.

A standing ovation.

Oh my gosh! She felt so exhilarated. So unbelievably happy.

When Roarke raised her arm and pointed at her, the audience went wild.

Have mercy! They really liked her. She gushed like a schoolgirl.

In return, she raised Roarke's arm. The audience went equally wild. Oh dear.

As was tradition, her troupe surrounded the prince and princess and ushered them safely from the performance room.

A warm blanket was thrown around Sinderella's shoulders and Caprice quickly ushered her into another room away from the troupe.

"Merck wants to see you," Caprice said. Worry etched her voice. "And he sounds serious. Before you tell him where to take his disgusting offer, make sure he pays you first."

Ella had confided in Caprice about Merck's sexual insinuations and Caprice had been chilly with the man ever since, insisting they never

perform there again. But Ella had insisted they continue to accept
Merck and his generosity for as long as they could.

"I'll handle him, don't worry," Ella reassured her friend as Caprice
helped her into a gorgeous red velvet dress that made Ella look both
professional and sexy at the same time.

"Sweetie, I always worry about you. You're just like one of my
daughters to me and I don't like it when a dirty old man makes unclean
advances toward you. So please promise me you'll be very careful with
him tonight. I didn't like the smile he had on his face or the way his
fingers were groping inside his pants while he watched you and that
stranger performing."

"That's why we're here, Caprice. To make our audience horny."

Ella winked as she slipped on a pair of red high heels and headed
for the door.

Caprice grabbed Ella by the elbow stopping her short.

"Sin, you're not taking me seriously."

Geez, she'd never seen her friend this agitated before.

"Okay, I promise. I will be careful. Really." She patted the woman's
hand and Caprice reluctantly let go of her.

"Thanks for worrying about me," Ella soothed. "I'll make sure I get
the money before I kick his ass."

"Maybe I should come with you?"

Caprice's frostiness toward Merck wouldn't help the situation. "No
you stay here and wait with the crew. I'll be back soon."

Even though she'd reassured Caprice she'd be fine, uneasiness
swooped around Ella as she walked down the deserted hallway to his
personal office where she usually collected the cash from Merck.

The wooden oak door stood wide open and she readjusted her
mask before knocking and entering. She found Merck dressed in a dark
gray smoking jacket and matching pants, standing at the far side of the
rectangle-shaped room looking out the night-darkened window and
puffing on a stinky cigar.

Overhead a crystal chandelier sparkled splashes of bright light against the sultry red walls, tanned leather sofa and the giant, sleek mahogany office desk.

"Ah, beautiful Sinderella. Please come in. Come in." The gray-haired man of seventy smiled and waved her in.

"I hope you were pleased with tonight's performance," Ella said as she took a few steps inside, trying hard to appear confident and strong despite the bulge pressing at the older man's pants when he strolled toward her.

"Please, have a seat. I'll pour you a drink. How about a sherry? I've just had it imported from Jerez in Spain especially for you."

"I'd be pleased to have a glass, Merck." But she'd rather stand.

Despite her uneasiness, she came farther into the room. It was tradition that they share a drink before talking business. Asking for the money due her performers was always the worst part of being boss. But the members of her crew depended on her to get what was rightfully theirs and she'd never failed them.

Ella watched as he poured the drinks, scrutinizing his every move to make sure he didn't slip any type of date-rape drug into her drink. Call her paranoid, but in her line of business, she knew it was better to be paranoid than sorry.

"Sinderella, I must say your show was exceptionally well done tonight." He handed her the drink in an exquisitely long-stemmed wineglass. She waited until he took a few sips.

"I'm glad to hear you and the audience enjoyed yourselves. We aim to please."

She took a taste of the fruity drink and sweetness exploded against her taste buds.

"Exquisite sherry, Merck. You have exceptional taste."

Merck grinned. Instincts and experience told her it wasn't a genuine smile and tendrils of fear curled through her confidence.

She'd learned in their relationship that flattery got more help from Merck.

"How did you enjoy the new Prince Charming?" he asked. The question caught her totally off guard. "I was sure you'd pick me, Sinderella."

He'd moved closer. Way too close for comfort.

"I..." How did she tell a seventy-year-old man that she didn't pick him because she just wasn't impressed with him? And if she wasn't impressed, then the audience wouldn't be either.

"I apologize if someone gave you the idea you would be picked, Merck."

Blue cigar smoke twirled from his cigar and stung her eyes. She resisted the urge to move away from him, opting not to show him how uncomfortable she was getting. "But I'm the one who makes the final decisions."

He pouted. "I volunteered long before my friend Roarke did."

Oh for Pete's sake! He sounded as if he were a spoiled child.

"I've decided I want to be your Prince Charming tonight, Sinderella." He reached for her arm, but she managed to step away just in time.

"I'm sorry, Merck. But the performance for tonight is over. I am here to collect our payment."

"And what if I told you I'm not paying until you allow me to fuck you."

Bastard.

"I'd say you'd be insulting the group of Sinderella and we'd have to withhold any further performances until payment is rendered," she said firmly.

Gosh, why couldn't she be this bold with her stepmother and stepsisters? Because she was hiding behind the mask, that's why. Life was always easier when she pretended to be someone else.

His lips twisted with contempt. "Well, then. How's about a little kiss. Your performance with Roarke has gotten me so horny. You let him kiss you. I want to kiss you too."

"Kisses are out of the question, Merck. As I said—"

She cried out in surprise as Merck lunged and grabbed her by the arm, yanking her against his body. For an old guy he sure was strong!

"What the hell is the matter with you?" She tried to jerk away, but his grip tightened. His eyes seemed glazed and not at all normal. It looked as if he were in some kind of a trance.

She swallowed frantically at the panic climbing into her throat and shivered in revulsion as he rubbed his engorged erection against her thigh.

"I knew you'd like that cock, teasing, little slut," he growled. She grimaced at his acrid cigar smelling breath.

"Let go of me!"

Mercy! She couldn't believe this was happening. Couldn't believe how paralyzed she suddenly felt. She should be kicking him, struggling, but she could barely breathe.

"Merck, please. I'm tired. Just—"

"Oh but, no, I've just begun," he snarled.

Suddenly he pushed her. Hard. Ella gasped as she sailed backward, landing on the couch with a soft bounce. Before she could react, he'd dropped on top of her, pinning her beneath him, his heavy weight knocking the breath out of her lungs.

Oh, my God! She couldn't even scream for help, let alone gasp for air. Terror unlike anything she'd ever experienced swooped around her.

"Oh, sweet Sinderella. I want to put my cock into your tight pussy. I want to fuck your brains out."

Get off me! Her mind screamed. She could barely suck in a breath. The bastard felt like a cement block on top of her. His erection burned into her lower belly and she felt totally helpless as she lay trapped beneath him. He'd even ensnared her arms or she would have been scratching frantically at his eyes, his face, anything to get him off of her.

"A kiss. Just as you gave Roarke. And then I want to suck on those big nipples and your juicy pussy just like Roarke did. Nice and sweet, I bet."

Her eyes widened with disgust.

"Oh yeah, Roarke was bragging when I talked to him in the dressing room. He told me how I should taste your sweet lips and how the cream from your cunt drugged him. How good he felt with your mouth wrapped around his cock. How he wanted the both of us to get to know you better after the performance."

No way! There was no way Roarke would ever say something like that!

Merck's face drew closer.

"You'd like that wouldn't you, Sinderella? Having two Prince Charmings fucking you?"

His obscene breath seeped into her lungs.

Please someone help me!

She shivered as his grubby hand trailed up her inner thigh. Nausea rippled through her belly as he cupped her pussy.

"Let me see how wet you are for Prince Charming, sweet Sinderella. It'll be over fast. You've made me so horny. I'll just stick my cock into your cunt."

"Get the fuck off her, Merck, or I will kill you!"

Merck's body stiffened at the sound of Roarke's harsh voice and Ella said a silent thank you for her prince coming to her rescue.

"Oh, my God!" Caprice whispered. Her voice was laced with the same horror Ella was experiencing.

When the man didn't move fast enough off her, Roarke gripped Merck's shoulders and he literally picked the man up and stood him on his feet.

"Pay the women what you owe them and leave her the fuck alone!"

"Hey, come on. It's not like she's your girlfriend." Merck laughed uneasily as he brushed at his clothing.

The muscles in Roarke's jaws twitched angrily but he said nothing. He merely stared at Merck in disgust.

"Fine." Merck's hand slipped into a side pocket of his smoking jacket and pulled out a sizeable envelope. "It's all there."

"It better be." Roarke snapped the envelope away. "Now get out of my face before I do something you'll be sorry about...if you're lucky to wake up."

"Fuck you, Roarke," Merck grumbled, and then stomped off.

"Sweetie, are you all right." Caprice was suddenly sitting on the sofa beside her, enveloping Ella in her embrace. "Thank God, Roarke came with me. I told you Merck was up to no-good."

"I'm okay, really," Ella whispered, quite thankful for Caprice's strong arms holding her tight.

"Caprice," Roarke said gently. "I think you'd better get the money to the troupe and tell them to leave. There won't be any more performances Merck's house in the future."

Caprice nodded and pulled away. Her friend looked totally defiant and ready to fight if Ella didn't agree.

"He's right. We can't come here again. Not after what happened. Please don't tell the others about what just happened," Ella whispered, feeling shame heat her cheeks as Roarke frowned at her in the background. She avoided his gaze.

Oh damn! Now she really didn't want him to find out her true identity. He'd think she was a whore.

"You've done nothing wrong," Caprice reassured, and smiled warmly. "You have nothing to be ashamed of."

But she did feel ashamed. A man had literally thrown himself all over her without her heeding the warning signs. She'd been stupid to come in there alone.

"Let's please just forget this happened, okay?" She tried to smile at both of them, but her lips just kind of wobbled.

"Okay. I'll go give everyone their share," Caprice whispered, and let Ella go from her embrace.

"Thank you. I'll stay here for a few moments," Ella replied. She needed to get her bearings.

Caprice nodded. She looked at Roarke, and then nodded as if to say to herself Ella would be safe with him.

"Are you sure you're all right?" Roarke asked after Caprice left the room. The softness with which he spoke brought tears to Ella's eyes and she suddenly realized the full impact of what had almost happened. She could have been raped by Merck!

"I...I'm fine," she said as he sat down on the couch beside her, a severe frown on his face. His body warmth wrapped snugly around her, making her feel just a little bit safe and secure.

"You're shivering."

"Just adrenaline. I'm sure it'll go away in a few minutes. I do have to say thank you," she said. "I know what you must be thinking. How it looked. I mean I've never seen him act quite that way. He's insinuated things in the past and I've told him I'm not interested, but I never thought..."

"No man should force himself on a woman. If there hadn't been witnesses, he'd be dead now."

Ella blinked at the fierceness in his voice.

"I'm sorry. He must be drunk... I didn't mean to break up your friendship—"

"Christ, woman! He's no friend. And don't make excuses for him! Do you always accept blame for other people's stupidity?" He inhaled and shoved a hand through his hair.

Oh boy, he was really pissed off. Even when he was mad he looked sexy.

"I'm sorry. I shouldn't have yelled at you. He's a disgrace to mankind. I'm glad I've seen his true colors. Although, I'd rather it have been under different circumstances."

"Spoken like a true gentleman." She smiled.

"Or a true prince. Which leads me to why I was looking for you."

His green eyes glittered fiercely as he held out his hand. She spied the nipple ring with the pretty glass slipper nestled in the palm of his hand.

"You dropped it again after the performance. I thought you'd be needing it."

"Thank you." When she picked it up, her fingertips blazed as she touched his flesh.

"Would you like me to see you to your car?"

"No, I'm fine."

He nodded and an uneasy silence stretched between them.

"I should go now," she said. Yes, she should leave before she told him something she shouldn't. Despite her need to go, she couldn't move. "I guess I should personally thank you for agreeing to be my Prince Charming tonight."

Back off, Ella. Dangerous territory. Get out now while you still have a chance.

Her breath halted in her lungs as he suddenly reached up and caressed the bite he'd given her earlier on her neck. His intimate touch created sparkles of warmth. In all the excitement, she'd forgotten about the bite. Realized she'd have to find a way to cover it up tomorrow at work so he wouldn't see it.

"I apologize if I went too far. I just couldn't resist you."

Ella swallowed. "I...I've never had better," she admitted truthfully.

"I know you're upset about Merck. Maybe I should take you back to my place until you've calmed down."

Oh, how she'd love to go back to his place.

"No, I'm sorry. I'm sort of interested in someone." *You idiot! Tell him you're interested in him! Tell him he's everything you've ever dreamed of. Everything you've ever fantasized about. Only better.*

"Sort of interested? Meaning?"

"He's engaged."

"But he's not married. Maybe you would still have a chance with him if you told him your true feelings? I am assuming he doesn't know?"

"No," she admitted, wondering how in the world they'd gotten onto this subject.

"You should tell him. He may feel the same way about you. Maybe he's very attracted to you. You're a beautiful woman."

Oh my gosh. Roarke thinks I'm beautiful? Or does he think Sinderella is beautiful?

"Without the mask, I'm different," she admitted.

"With or without the mask, you're still attractive. You still taste the same. Talk the same. Act the same. Sexy. Beautiful."

Warmth scuttled over her cheeks.

"You're blushing."

"I'm sorry."

"No, don't be. It's very sexy."

Blushing is sexy? Her breathing went shallow.

His intense gaze held her captive. "Does this guy you're interested in know that you do this Sinderella show?"

"I've never told him."

"Why not?"

Was he persistent or what?

"Because he might not understand?"

"Hmm. How do you know unless you tell him?"

"It's too big of a chance to take. If I tell him, then he'll know what I do. If he doesn't understand..." If he didn't understand, he'd laugh at her. He'd think of her as being a big fool. She'd be devastated. For Roarke not to know might be easier for both of them.

His hand came up and a thumb caressed one corner of her mouth, making her heart pick up speed and her insides quiver with need.

"Is he the jealous type?"

She'd never really thought about that. Was Roarke the jealous type? Would he consider her a slut for having oral sex with strange men? All her fantasies had been about him loving her. Sinderella hadn't been in the picture. Maybe because she had been fantasizing and not really considering reality. That's why she'd never seriously thought about it.

"I don't know if he is," she answered truthfully.

"Why not tell me why you sing and dance and perform in such a luscious story? Then I could tell you from a man's perspective if he might have a problem with it."

Here was her chance to find out exactly what Roarke would think about her. It was an opportunity she might never have again.

"There is one main reason why I perform."

In answer he quirked an eyebrow. The sight made her belly flutter. He looked so sexy when he did that.

"Being?"

She didn't know why she hesitated. But she did. It wasn't as if she had anything to lose. She actually felt quite comfortable speaking to Roarke with her face hidden. It seemed as if he were suddenly a good friend, a confidant. Hell! He really had no idea he was talking to his klutzy coworker.

"I feel free when I perform," she admitted. "During my formative years I put all my time into working toward a career. It left me with no social skills with men and so now I hide behind my mask." There she'd said it. She'd bared her heart for him and it hadn't even hurt.

"I see." Was that disappointment in his voice? "I'd say the whole thing lies on the premise if this man you're interested in is a jealous type or not. If he is the jealous type, then he would have a very hard time with it, especially if he knew other men were sexually satisfying you and he was at home waiting in the wings so to speak. That wouldn't go over too well."

Shit! How could she find out if Roarke was the jealous type? She could come straight out and ask him. Couldn't she?

"If he's not the jealous type," he continued. "Then your relationship probably wouldn't work out. It means he doesn't care enough or love you enough."

"Oh." Now she was more confused than ever.

"But if the man were me..."

Ella's breath halted in her lungs as she anxiously awaited his answer.

"But he isn't me so you wouldn't need my opinion on the matter."

Her hopes deflated.

"You said you had a main reason. That means you have other reasons?"

"Well, actually, yes. A very important reason. The money I make I donate anonymously to some local charities for young girls and women."

His eyes widened for a split second and he looked as if he might be surprised at her answer, but then he smiled easily.

"I'd say that's a noble and understandable cause that your man would certainly understand."

Suddenly Caprice's voice echoed down the hall. She was coming back to see how Ella was doing.

"I really have to go."

"So you wish to remain a mystery to me?"

God! Of course, she didn't want to remain a mystery to him. Especially after what he'd just said about understanding why she wished to keep her identity a secret.

But she had no choice. She didn't want to break his engagement. Whatever gave her the idea that she could? She'd seen his fiancée's picture. She was beautiful. Voluptuous. A looker. And his fiancée didn't have the Sinderella skeleton in her closet like Ella did.

"Ella, come on, honey. I'll walk you to the car." Caprice stood in the doorway.

Before he could say anything else, she headed for the door. She half expected him to follow as she left with Caprice.

He didn't.

Disappointment rocked her, and by the time her friend had her safely tucked inside the car and waved goodbye to her, Ella allowed the tears to burst free.

God! She'd really made a mess of her life, hadn't she?

Tonight she'd had oral sex with the man of her fantasies, had almost gotten raped by that bastard Merck and now she was letting her Prince Charming go. She was simply no good for his career. That is if he truly had wanted her and not Sinderella as he'd said.

.. ⁓ ..

ROARKE LISTENED TO the grandfather clock in the hallway ring the twelve bells.

Midnight.

For real this time.

Frustration grabbed at him. Instincts told him he should follow her home and confront her.

Fuck! Why had he allowed her to go so easily? Because Merck's house wasn't the place to tell her how much he wanted her.

He'd wait. But not for long.

He turned to leave when a shimmer on the floor caught his eye.

Sinderella's nipple ring with the glass slipper. She must have dropped it again on her way out.

Roarke frowned and picked up the delicate item.

Now he understood how Prince Charming must have felt when the real Cinderella had left the Prince's Ball.

Shitty. Real fucking shitty.

Chapter Six

WHEN SHE'D FIRST COME to work at Cinder her stepfamily had stuck her in an office in the doldrums of the hospital. They thought she'd be intimidated at being told there hadn't been any more office space in the mainstream area of the hospital her father had created. Instead, they'd accommodated her with a spot in the basement. In an empty room.

She hadn't been put off. Not in the least.

She craved solitude and her cozy office allowed her the quiet she needed to do her paperwork quickly and efficiently. Of course, the way she'd decorated it had helped. She'd done it in one weekend. Had painted the back brick wall in a soft yellow and done the rest of her office in a cheerful wallpaper that made it look like an artist had dumped red, green and yellow paint everywhere.

Of course, her stepmother had been horrified, but Ella had forced herself to take a stand. Had refused to submit to having a painter come in and drown her artistic endeavor with puke green paint as everyone else's office had been decorated in.

As if she could call a bile green color as being decorative. She'd further mutinied by purchasing a gorgeous desk with steel legs topped with a thick sheet of clear glass. It housed her bright red designer computer. She'd also lugged into the colorful mix her comfy yet tattered ergonomic computer chair. Sleek white mini blinds hung on the wired glass window of her office door, insuring her privacy.

Lining the wide hallway just outside her door, she kept her huge floor to ceiling filing cabinet with her patients' files.

Speaking of patients, she'd just been given China Smith's lab results and was in the process of scrutinizing it when Roarke's soft voice zipped through the air making her breath still in her chest.

"Why don't you turn that frown upside down?"

Her head snapped up and she watched, transfixed by those gorgeously wide shoulders, as he strolled into her office and stopped in front of her glass desk.

The muscles in her lower belly clenched wickedly as his masculine scent swept around her, capturing her, making her tremble with fierce need.

"I just looked in on China. She's doing exceptionally well. She can be released soon," he said.

It was late in the day and he had that sexy stubble of beard growing. God! It made him look so much like a bad boy!

Ella cleared her suddenly dry throat.

"I know. I've just been looking at her latest test results. She and the baby are going to make it."

"And the reason for your frown is?"

"She's homeless unless she returns to her pimp, which she is considering. I'm racking my brains trying to get her some help. If I can get her deemed as an adult and get her welfare, she can find an apartment—"

"There are other options."

"If you're talking about sending her back to her family, that's totally out of the question. She ran away in the first place because her stepfather was sexually abusing her."

Now it was Roarke's turn to frown. "We can get her into foster care."

"Won't happen. I already mentioned it, and she doesn't trust adults."

"She trusted you..."

"Only because she heard about me through a good friend, or she wouldn't have come here. She trusts no one in any type of authority figure. Her stepfather is a cop...she's afraid if she does trust any adult in authority, the same thing will happen to her again."

"And being a prostitute is different?" he snapped. His eyes blazed with a sudden burst of anger that rattled Ella.

"Her pimp is fifteen," she explained.

Roarke swore softly.

She wasn't normally a person who pried into other people's business, but the look of anguish flaring across Roarke's face made her bold.

"Sounds to me like China's story has hit a nerve. You care to tell me about it?"

"You want to tell me why you're wearing a silk scarf around your neck?"

She froze at his question.

"The scarf makes you look quite sexy," he continued. "But personally, I prefer to see your neck bare."

She found herself searching his green eyes. The hurt was still there, but it sparkled amidst other emotions.

Lust. Desire. Sexual need.

"Do you always use changing the subject as a self-defense mechanism?" she whispered, suddenly understanding Roarke the man. He wasn't as complicated as she'd thought. There was another side to him just as she'd suspected.

"You're a quick study, aren't you?" he grumbled, but she noted the sweet pull of amusement tipping his lips.

"Only when you show me your tender side," she admitted. She found herself answering his smile and felt her old glasses move down the bridge of her nose as they always seemed to do lately. Quickly she pressed the metal frame against the bridge of her nose and caught him watching her. Suddenly she could barely breathe.

"You look really sexy when you do that, Ella."

"I do?"

His comment totally caught her off guard.

"Very sexy."

Oh dear.

He smiled. "I can get China into a home for unwed mothers. I have pull there. I run it."

"Oh? You run it?"

He didn't strike her as the type of a man who'd actually do something like that. Obviously she had a lot to learn about him.

"You sound surprised that I actually have a heart."

His eyes appeared to have darkened as he looked at her.

"Um..." Gosh she didn't know what to say.

He turned and headed back for the door again. For a moment she thought she'd offended him by not saying anything and now he was leaving, but he didn't go.

He stared at the closed door for a moment and said softly, "You really should get a lock for the door."

Her heart thundered at the sound of his thick voice. He turned around and she instantly recognized that look. The searing look that made her face flame.

He wanted her.

As he came toward her, she felt nervous. Boy, did she feel nervous!

His big size made the room seem awfully small.

"Wouldn't want us to get interrupted."

Her eyes widened at his statement.

Sweet shit! He wouldn't try anything in her office, would he? Her pussy tightened at that thought.

"I guess I should tell you the truth about why I accepted this position at Cinder."

Ella blinked in confusion. One minute he acted sexy as sin, the next minute he was in confession mode.

"I know your father left you as a co-owner, but I don't feel disloyal telling you that I took this job strictly for the money and I don't really give two shits about the rich snobs who Cinder targets."

"You don't?"

"No, and I'm pretty sure you don't either."

He slipped his lab coat off and let it fall to the floor. He began to unbutton his shirt.

Oh my goodness!

"I need the money for a home I help run with my mother. The state only gives us a certain amount and we have a tendency of using it up before the end of the allocated period. The government doesn't seem to realize how much prenatal care girls really need when they are pregnant. So I took this job to help finance my dream."

"Which is?"

He shrugged out of his shirt. She couldn't seem to keep her eyes off his naked chest. Couldn't forget the feel of the hard bunch of chest muscles she'd touched last night.

"A soft place for teenage mothers to fall is our dream. A soft place my mother didn't have forty years ago when she was at the age of fourteen raped by a neighbor. Scandal forced her onto the streets."

"You were a product of rape?"

"No, my brother was. When she was on the streets, a pimp got his clutches into her. He forced her to give him up after he was born. She's never been able to find him. He brainwashed her, stole her self-esteem and used her for almost five years before she ran off with a john of hers. They got married and I'm one of two kids they had. My mom was one of the lucky ones."

Ella swallowed. "I'm so sorry about what happened to her when she was young."

"Don't be."

His fingers were now unbuttoning the stud at the waist of his jeans. Oh dear!

"My mother always says bad things happen for a reason. You just have to search for the positive side and use it to your advantage. If things hadn't happened the way they did, then my mother wouldn't have told me her stories and I wouldn't have this passion to help unwed mothers. My girls wouldn't have A Soft Place To Fall."

"That's the charity—" She cut herself off. She'd been about to tell him that's one of the charities she donated her Sinderella money to.

The sound of his zipper made her return her attention to his waist. His jeans were now open, riding low on his hips, exposing a tight pair of black underwear and a delicious arrow of crisp, brown curls.

Ella blew out a tense breath.

"But don't let those she-devil stepsisters or stepmother know, they just might have a heart attack that their colleague might actually have a life outside of Cinder, unlike themselves."

He stood very close to her now.

"I'm good at keeping secrets," she found herself whispering.

"I know you are."

His hand was at her neck, untying the knot on her scarf. Before she could even simulate thoughts in her mind to find some form of protest, her neck was bare.

Roarke's eyes blazed. "Just as I suspected. Sinderella, I presume." He stroked a lone finger along her sore hickey, the brand he'd left on her neck last night.

His breathing seemed rough now. Uneven.

Her heart pounded. Roarke knew her secret!

"How did you know? When did you start to suspect?"

"You had me the instant I first heard you singing. Deep down, somewhere inside me, I knew it was you, but I just couldn't believe sensuous Sinderella was the same as sexy-as-sin Ella, the woman I've been craving to fuck since the first day I saw you."

Ella's cheeks flushed with heat.

"What about your fiancée?"

"Actually she's my younger sister who lives overseas. We had pictures done the last time she came for a visit. I used one of them."

Holy! He was unattached. There was nothing keeping her from pursuing him. The idea seemed overwhelming. Almost too good to be true.

"You didn't name any names last night when you mentioned the charities you donate to, but I'm assuming you are the anonymous donor for A Soft Place to Fall."

"I am," she confessed.

"My girls appreciate your help. We'd be hurting without your generosity, Ella."

His fierce gaze never left her face as his finger moved lazily up her flushed cheek to caress her chin. She trembled at his soft touch.

"I can think of one hell of a good way to thank you for donating to our cause."

"I don't expect any thanks. I do it because I enjoy giving."

"And I enjoy receiving."

Sparks of hunger speared through her as he leaned down and his lips slid hungrily against hers. She couldn't even think to hesitate when he yanked her to her feet beside him.

His mouth remained erotically fused with hers, his tongue dueled with hers.

Hunger gnawed deep inside her empty cunt. His hard body pressed against hers, firing her arousal.

He broke the kiss. His eyes blazed as his fingers quickly opened her blouse. Her breasts were swelling against her bra. Cool air washed over her suddenly bare shoulders as he pulled the blouse off. His hot fingers curled beneath the elastic of her pants, his touch searing her skin, making her cry out at its intensity. With a quick, desperate tug, he had her pants down around her ankles. Then her thong underwear joined them.

He jerked both of them and her shoes off her feet.

She cried out as he lifted her and slammed her bare ass upon her cool, glass table. Reaching around her, he unclasped her bra and whipped it aside. They were both breathing roughly, the sounds shooting through her office like bullets. She could feel the slick juices escape her vagina, probably smearing her tabletop.

He spread her legs wide. Stepped between them. The sight of his heavily muscled chest just about made her come on the spot. His eyes were wild. So wild.

She watched as he slipped his jeans and underwear down over his hips releasing his cock.

Thick and long, the huge bald head flushed an angry purple. Her nipples hardened at the sight, her pussy creamed more.

"You're so fucking beautiful, Ella," his voice sounded strangled, heavy. His eyes glittered with lust. "I want you so fucking bad. I can't wait any longer. I've held myself back for so long. Pretending not to care just because I didn't want to mix business with pleasure. Too many months of fantasizing."

She fought for breath at his admission. He'd wanted her just as badly as she wanted him?

Oh yes! There was a God!

"I want to bind you. Whip you. Fuck you a hundred different ways. I want you to be my fantasy girl, Ella. Every day, every night."

Ella couldn't stop herself from moaning as she remembered her own fantasy scenes with the same themes.

"Last night when I saw Merck touching you against your will, I wanted to kill him. I don't want another man near you. I am the jealous type. I care too much about you to let another day go by without showing you how I've felt about you all this time. I want to be your man and your Prince Charming in your future Sinderella productions."

Her pussy spasmed as he stroked the long length of his cock. Her body heated with longing.

"You haven't officially been interviewed for the position of my Prince Charming," she teased.

"Then we'll do an interview now. You can let me know later if I passed. Lie back on the desk."

His unexpected order made her blink in confusion. This was happening way too fast. She could barely get her mind around the fact that she sat naked on her office desk in front of Roarke without her mask and his fierce, hungry gaze was zeroed in right between her legs.

"Trust me, sweet Sin."

She loved his nickname for her and did as he asked, lying backward on the table, the smooth, cool glass caressing her ass and back.

She yelped as his hot hands sidled around her ankles and he hoisted her legs up, spreading them as he placed them over his rock-hard shoulders.

"Play with your breasts," he ordered.

As he watched her, she did as he said. Her heart pounded out of control as she looked down at her two mounds and touched her sensitive nipples. She didn't wear her nipple rings today because her nipples were still so sensitive from Roarke's attentions last night.

The instant she pinched the tips, pleasure flared.

"Keep playing with yourself," he demanded.

She did. She watched her breasts swell and her nipples turn hard and rosy beneath his fierce stare and her intimate touches. She cried out as an unexpected finger smoothed over her clit, unleashing the carnal cravings lusting inside her. It took him only seconds and he had her on fire, her pussy soaked and aching to be filled, and her breaths reduced to cries.

With a growl he thrust inside her.

Deep. Hard. Intense.

Ella exploded. *Oh God! This feels too fucking good to be real!*

Erotic pleasure tore through her as Roarke's thick, powerful cock plunged in and out of her, making her breasts bounce wildly beneath her hands. Suctioning sounds split the air. The scent of her sex filled her nostrils.

"Oh yes! Roarke, fuck me! Fuck me harder!" she gasped, and kept pinching and tugging her sore nipples, tossing her head to and fro, thoroughly enjoying the carnal spasms making her tremble.

Suddenly from the corner of her eye she detected movement. Realized the office door had opened. Someone was standing there! Her stepmother! And her two evil stepsisters!

"Oh, God!" she cried out, stunned at the increasing arousal screaming through her at knowing the bitches were watching Roarke fuck her.

Another climax gripped her. Lust, raw and carnal roared through her. She closed her eyes and drowned in the pleasure that Roarke's wickedly delicious cock gave so freely. His finger continued to massage her ultrasensitive clit and he just kept pumping into her.

Hard and fierce just as she'd asked. Oh yes! Beautiful!

"Get the fuck out of here!" she heard Roarke growl at them. But he didn't miss a beat as he continued to pleasure her.

"This is shocking behavior!" her stepmother stuttered.

"What Ella and I do in the privacy of her own office is none of your fucking business. Get the fuck out! Now! And knock next time."

The slamming of the door barely registered as Roarke continued with his deliciously hard thrusts. Her pussy continued to spasm. Her body lost in a storm of pleasure.

"First thing we do is get a lock on that door," he ground out. His hips pumped faster, his cock roared in and out, driving Ella to more carnal sensations.

"I want you to be the woman of my fantasies, Ella, and I want to be the man in yours."

"You already are my fantasy man," she admitted.

He grinned that incredible sexy grin she loved, and when she started coming down from her third fantastic orgasmic high, she felt Roarke's hot jets of sperm filling her.

Epilogue

Several weeks later...

At the sound of the door to the examination room opening and closing softly, Ella bit down on the ball gag in her mouth with wicked anticipation.

Oh God! Roarke was here!

Roarke, who'd turned out to be a more fierce lover than even her wildest fantasy. After the day her stepmother and stepsisters had caught Roarke making love to her in her office, Ella had gloated at their envious looks.

He'd invited her to move in with him and they'd been practically and literally inseparable ever since. From that time on, she'd also learned that having people watching her have sex was only one of her many sexual fetishes. She enjoyed being whipped, craved being taken by Roarke compliments of the doggie style and loved having her nipples clamped.

By day they continued to work at Cinder Hospital catering to the rich and snobby, yet slowly implementing new rules using her part ownership in the hospital to loosen restrictions so Ella could care for low-income and homeless pregnant girls and women who needed them the most.

Some evenings she helped Roarke and his charming mother at A Soft Place To Fall. His father worked there also. He was a tall, older version of Roarke, extremely jovial and fun to be around. His mother was sweet and so affectionate that she felt safe and loved by the older woman who Ella believed would have been an ideal mother for herself.

A few nights a month she also continued being Sinderella with a disguised Roarke as her Prince Charming. Despite Merck not being involved any longer, the carnal act had expanded quickly based on word-of-mouth alone. They always closed to a standing ovation.

When Roarke got her alone, he continued to surprise her with a variety of delightful pleasures such as tonight when he'd brought her to one of the examination rooms at the hospital that contained a rigged-up gyno table where he'd instructed her in what to do to ready herself for him.

"All ready for your examination, Ella?" His deep voice ripped her back to the present and her pussy spasmed with excitement. She swallowed at the rustle of clothing being removed and blew out a shaky breath through her nose at the sound of his bare feet padding closer to her.

Her cheeks warmed as he suddenly stood beside the gyno table where he'd instructed her to strap her feet into the cool, silver stirrups and to lash restraints over and under her breasts securing her.

She inhaled a quivering breath as Roarke's hand smoothed over her wrist, bringing it to her side. The snap of Velcro quickly followed and she automatically pulled against her bond. Nothing budged. He did the same with her other wrist, binding her. Making her his captive. Putting her at his total mercy.

Oh boy.

"Are you okay?"

Ella nodded. Bondage was something she'd always wanted to try. Now she had the chance.

I trust you. Her body tingled at the warmth flooding through her. She was lusciously naked and ready for Roarke's intimate exam.

"Let's start with your breasts."

She whimpered around the gag as he looked at her full mounds. Her nipples responded immediately to his hungry gaze, blushing a beautiful burgundy color as they hardened.

"Very nice. I can see your breasts are in great condition."

Did she detect huskiness in his otherwise confident voice? For a moment he left her view, and when he came back he held a small whip in his hand.

Oh sweet mercy!

Her pussy contracted. Creamed in anticipation.

"Are you ready?"

She nodded. Braced herself.

The whishing sound of the whip sailed through the air. Pain snapped into her left nipple. She jerked in reaction. Watched her tip turn red with anger. Her tummy clenched. Her pussy grew warm.

Pulsed.

More lashes. This time on her breasts. Blistering heat mixed with pain. She bucked against her restraints with every lash.

Bright red stripes interlaced her globes. By the time he finished with her breasts they burned and her pussy was creaming up a storm.

"Are you horny, Ella?" His strangled question made her avert from his lusty gaze. Heat fused her face. Her body tightened with exquisite need.

"No answer? Hmm, I guess I'll have to examine your pussy."

Ella's thighs tightened with need as Roarke moved to the foot of the table. Her legs were spread wide. Her feet held captive by stirrups and her heart pumped madly at the anticipation in his green eyes when he noticed the wide base of the butt plug in her ass.

"Very nice, Ella," he complimented.

She bit against the ball gag as his hands glided softly along her inner thighs toward her pussy and her plugged anus.

A single finger smoothed over her clit, bringing instant pleasure.

"You're so fucking responsive, Ella," he groaned. She knew he loved the way she reacted so quickly to his touch. Knew it meant she craved him just as much as he yearned for her.

His finger dipped into her vagina, smoothing back and forth, massaging her G-spot until she shivered and whimpered beneath his sensual touches.

The pleasure built swiftly and she twisted against her restraints.

Please! Fuck me! Her mind screamed. God! She loved Roarke so much. Loved the things he did to her body, the sexy way he made her feel.

"Let's get rid of that butt plug so I can fuck your tight little ass, shall we?"

She nodded eagerly, her mind screaming at him to hurry. She'd always wanted to experience anal penetration, but hadn't had the nerve to ask. When he'd broached the subject several weeks ago, she readily agreed. She'd worn the various sizes of plugs. Allowing them to stretch her, to fill her, prepare her for him.

The last one, the huge one was just about as big as his cock and now lay buried inside her rear end.

"Before I fuck your tight little ass, I've got a present for you."

Her eyes widened as he produced a large, black glass wand. It looked to be about ten glorious inches long with a straight shaft at least two inches wide with one half-inch smooth swirls and dots webbed along the entire length. And the stylized, round glass head looked so wonderfully huge.

"I had it made just for you, sweet Sin. I call it the pleasure rod."

Heat spread through her as he dipped the glass wand between her legs. While he massaged her clit with the round head, she groaned at the pleasure the rod created.

A moment later she felt the sex toy pushing into her. Stretching her. Making her moan as the smooth ridges and dots caressed her insides.

He began to thrust it in and out of her. She arched her hips, silently demanding more pleasure. Wanting harder thrusts.

"You are insatiable, Ella. I love that about you. I love everything about you," Roarke groaned.

And then the glass wand stopped, and through her sexual haze, she heard the slurpy sounds of Roarke dipping his fingers into the jar of lubricant she'd noticed earlier on the nearby table when she'd first entered the exam room. She whimpered her excitement as he liberally applied the lube to his cock. Smearing every glorious inch of his thick, pulsing, rigid piece of flesh.

She found herself flushing as he leaned forward, felt the butt plug move. Strange sensations she rather liked gripped her anus as he slowly pulled the object from her body.

His breathing had quickened. Her heart raced with anticipation. She groaned around the ball gag as a generously lubed finger thrust inside her ass, pressing past her now loosened sphincter muscle. Despite his finger feeling so small compared to the huge plug, incredible sensations wrapped around her as he moved in an erotically slow exploration. He groaned. "I can't wait to fuck your sweet little ass."

The glass wand was on the move again, slipping across her engorged clit with a delightfully hard rub.

Sweet pleasure flared in her pussy.

"Your virgin ass isn't going to be that way for much longer, Sexy Sin."

Roarke slipped another generously lubed finger into her anus making her moan at the foreign intrusion of two hot, slippery fingers widening her. Invading her.

He slipped the glass wand into her tight cunt. The large ball stretching her. Filling her soaked pussy.

In no time flat he had her moaning at a gentle yet insistent rhythm of both her channels being gloriously filled. Her thighs clenched tightly. Her body hummed.

Oh wow! It felt unbelievable.

"I can tell by your wide eyes, you are pleased."

Pleased was an understatement! She bit down on the ball gag as a third lubed finger thrust into her tender ass.

Oh God! His fingers were stretching her ass so incredibly full. The glass wand slurped in and out of her snug cunt making Ella moan beneath the dual thrusts.

Perspiration dotted her skin. Her harsh breaths came fast and tortured.

"And now, Sweet Sin, brace yourself."

She whimpered as he withdrew his fingers with a slurp and guided his angry-looking, stiff cock closer to her splayed-out body. When the hot, lubricated cock head pushed against her sphincter, she couldn't help but cry against the gag in wonder at the odd sensation.

Keeping the glass rod impaled inside her soaked cunt, he pushed his long, thick cock into her ass. Immediately his face became an image of tortured pleasure. And he'd barely penetrated her.

"Oh yes, Ella. Your ass is so tight."

He pushed into her ass farther. She felt her eyes widen in wonder at the sudden burst of pleasure-pain.

He'd warned her about it. Warned her to simply keep herself relaxed and breathe into it. And that's exactly what she did. She focused on the pleasure-pain while he kept his hungry gaze glued to her face, to her eyes, watching her carefully.

She knew he searched for her safe signal of three rapid eye blinks for him to stop if she felt she couldn't endure it. But she didn't want him to stop. The exquisite intermingling of pleasure mixed with sweet pain had her craving for more.

His thick cock filled her ass—her muscles eagerly gripped his hard, hot length. Her thighs clenched as his hard cock burrowed deeper.

Sweet mercy but he was long! She could feel every hard, delicious inch of his rigid flesh buried deep inside her.

He kept the wand on the move. His thrusts becoming quicker, fiercer. The smooth glass ridges seared into her vagina, making her forget exactly how big an intruder his cock felt as he impaled her ass.

Without warning he pulled his cock out and speared back into her again. She whimpered at the brilliant onslaught. The dual thrusts became faster. Erotic sensations flared. Her body tightened, flared with wicked pleasure.

She closed her eyes and breathed into the glowing eroticism as it exploded all around her.

Sweet carnal sensations.

She convulsed beneath his hard thrusts. Exquisite spasms tore through her. She could barely assimilate what was happening.

"Beautiful, Sin! Just fucking beautiful!" Roarke's pleased voice ground out so far away.

As he came inside her, she simply allowed herself to float into the erotic bliss, all the while her mind kept repeating over and over again, *Oh yes, Fairy Godmother, I believe.*

I believe in the magic of miracles because my miracle came true.

For more ebooks and print books please visit
http://www.janspringer.com
MINI CATALOG
<u>Boxed Sets</u>

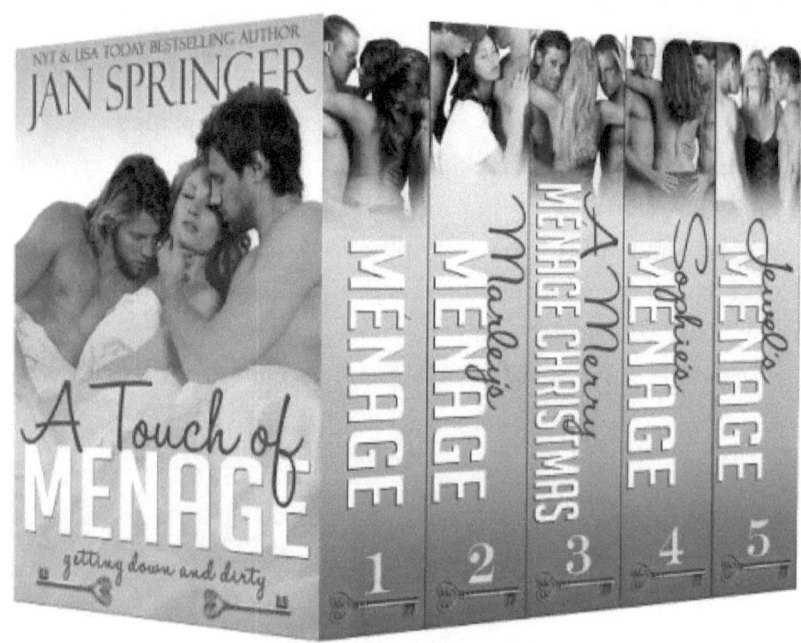

***SIX Erotic Romance Ménage Stories! INCLUDES A BONUS
MENAGE EBOOK***

STEP INTO THE KEY CLUB's Ménage Nights where naughty
fantasies come true and two men are hotter than one. Includes FIVE
bestselling The Key Club stories; Ménage, Marley's Ménage, A Merry
Ménage Christmas, Sophie's Ménage and Jewel's Ménage.

BONUS Ménage BOOK "Cowboys for Christmas" book 1 of
Jan's new Cowboys Online series. Jennifer Jane is getting THREE
Cowboys for Christmas ~ What more could a girl want?

Jennifer Jane Watson has spent the past ten Christmases in a maximum-security prison. The last thing she expects is to get early parole along with a job on a secluded Canadian cattle ranch serving Christmas holiday dinners to three of the sexiest cowboys she's ever met!

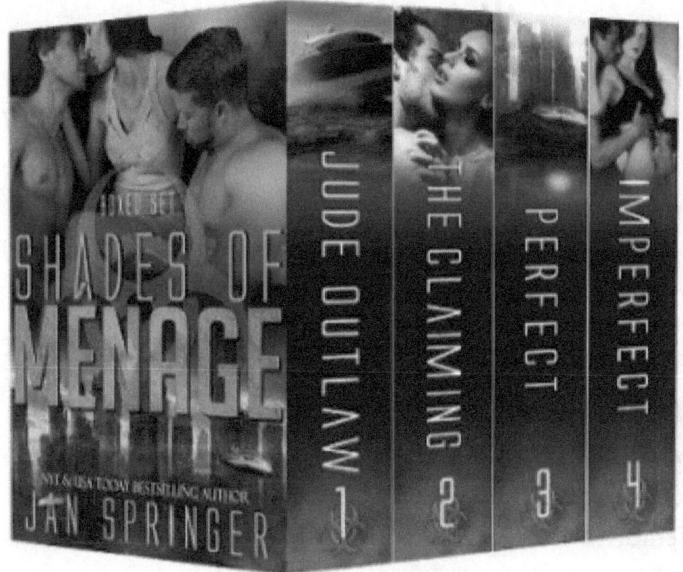

Shades of Ménage Boxed Set: Four Book Romance Ménage Collection

A FAST-ACTING VIRUS has killed a majority of the world's female population. Women's rights are stripped away and The Claiming Law is created, allowing groups of men to stake a claim on a female—as their sensual property.

After five years of fighting in the Terrorist Wars, the Outlaw brothers are coming home to declare ownership on the women they love...and they'll do it any way they can in Jude Outlaw and The Claiming.

PLUS

In the future...for population control, each human is embedded with a microchip that suppresses the urge to mate.

Centuries later...A rebel group of young doctors are secretly tampering with their microchips and experimenting with intimacy. Now they search for allies who can help them with their cause – to eventually free humanity in the Dystopian Romance Ménage stories "Perfect" & "Imperfect"

Stand-alone titles

• • ❦ • •

TOYGASM (CONTEMPORARY Erotic Romance Ménage)

It's a case of mistaken identity when identical twin brothers Josh and Jode Midnight, owners of Sexy Toys, show up for an erotic photo shoot of their toys with famous nude model Cammie Creek.

Cammie believes the two well-hung hunks are the men she's supposed to pose with. Usually she doesn't mix business with pleasure but when they're seducing her right in front of the cameras and delivering the best orgasms she's ever experienced, she can't resist turning them into her personal sex toys.

Josh and Jode can't get enough of Cammie—hot lust, sizzling toys and the best sex they've ever had. But how will she react when she discovers they're actually her bosses and that they fell in love with her before they'd even met her?

• • ❦ • •

EDIBLE DELIGHTS (CONTEMPORARY Erotic Romance Ménage)

Years ago, Allie Masters lost herself in the scorching passion of a ménage a trois relationship with her two striking bosses. In order to regain her independence, she walked away. Max and Nick were very fulfilled with their gorgeous redheaded assistant. The lovemaking was breathtaking and both friends willingly shared the woman they wanted to spend the rest of their lives with. And then she left. Now Max and Nick have decided it's time to seduce Allie back into their lives.

• • ❦ • •

HER CAPTIVE (CONTEMPORARY Erotic Romance)

Her perfect lover...

Modern day pirate Morgan Black's life has always been immersed in the violent and traditional ways of piracy. When her family's arch enemy puts a hit on her family, Morgan knows there's one sure way to lift the hit; she must kidnap their enemy's sexy grandson and literally force a union between the two warring families. Night after night, wrapped in Roman's strong arms, she can't deny the searing attraction blazing between them. Nor can she deny he now holds her heart as well as her life in his hands.

His dream angel...

When Roman Prince's captor offers him her luscious body, fierce desire ignites, melting his usually tight self-control. Lust quickly turns to love as he enjoys their naughty sexual trysts more than he knows he should. But how will he react when he discovers he's been kidnapped, not for a ransom, but for his sperm?

• • ✦ • •

LET'S GET PHYSICAL (Contemporary Erotic Romance with ménage scenes)

When the local swingers' club throws a Medical Fetish Night Before Xmas party for charity, Roxie learns that scrumptious blue-collar worker Evan Johnston will be playing doctor...

And he's offering one lucky lady an erotic sexual exam—along with a sizzling ménage e trois.

Roxie is desperate to be his patient. There's no better way to intimately know the guy who's stolen her heart than by hopping on the gyno table for the hottest physical of her life.

Passionate Ink (Shapeshifter Erotic Romance - m/f)

Tattoo artist Catalina Brown falls head-over-orgasms for the stranger who asks for a tentacle tattoo on his cock. Normally mixing business with pleasure isn't her thing, but he's a sexual desire she can't resist, especially when she becomes immersed in wicked-hot artistic highs as she tattoos every succulent inch. So why does he seem too good to be true?

Octoposeidon shape shifter Calder Croft catches the female's succulent scent when she passes his California marina, and he can't ignore the ravishing way she fires his blood. Only after meeting her, he's stunned to discover she has no idea she's a shifter about to come into her Change. It takes all his self-control to keep from taking the sexy female he craves right on the spot. He has to tell her the truth about her heritage. Will she accept her birthright as a shifter or will she succumb to madness and deny their forever?

Bared to Him (ShapeShifter Paranormal Erotic Romance m/f)
Sequel to Passionate Ink

Human by day, and a tentacle shape shifter by night, Gray Wagner, is the last male that Miranda Bolton would ever dream of falling in love with. He's an irritating, arrogant male who teases her to no end. With a human father and an Octo mother, Miranda knows she has a good chance at becoming a tentacle shifter just like Gray. When she can't stop fantasizing about the sexy well-hung male, she knows she's about to enter the Change and suddenly Gray becomes the only male she wants to mate with and she'll make sure she gets what she craves...

Alaskan custom boat maker, Gray Wagner, promised Miranda's dad that he would keep his daughter safe during their weeklong ocean voyage to attend a mutual friend's wedding in California, but Miranda's succulent scent is driving Gray to distraction. He knows he shouldn't be thinking about doing all the dirty and delicious things he wants to do to her, but all his promises to Miranda's father disintegrate when Miranda shifts and Gray goes primal...

Sexual Release (Fantasy Erotic Romance Ménage)

Princess Mica of Azar is approaching her thirtieth birthday. It's a time when an Azarian woman begins her cravings for Sexual Release with one or more males. Because she lives all alone on her planet, Mica has created a very special birthday present for herself—two full-grown stud clones made in the images of her childhood friends, Dakota and Nathan, humans who were captured and taken away as slaves years ago.

They were her best friends yet she was forbidden to love them, compliments of Azar's Purity Law. With her newly created sexy clone studs, she is planning to release the fires that rage within.

Dakota and Nathan have finally managed to escape their captors and return to make Princess Mica their mate. But how will she react when she discovers they've taken the place of her precious clones and that they won't be taking orders from her?

Reader Advisory: Story contains a scene that includes male/male erotic interaction.

. . ❧ . .

THE FIRE WITHIN (FUTURISTIC Erotic Romance m/f)

When Sex Squad Detective Sky Kelley informs her fiancé, Detective Jim O'Brien that she wants to wait until they're married before they have sex, he dumps her! Angry and defiant at his rejection, Sky undertakes a dangerous mission to the dark sensual world of sex slave training on one of Saturn's pleasure moons.

When Jim discovers Sky has volunteered for the mission, he's enraged. She's too pure and innocent for such a naughty assignment and he has no choice but to follow her. However, Sky isn't anybody's damsel in distress and she's going to prove it in ways Jim has only dreamed about...

Series
Pleasure Bound Series (Futuristic Erotic Romance m/f)

• • ☙ • •

PLEASURE BOUND SERIES
Futuristic Erotic Romance
A Hero's Welcome - Book One
A Hero Escapes - Book Two
A Hero Betrayed - Book Three
A Hero's Kiss - Book Four
A Hero Needed - Book Five
(Book 5 is loosely connected to this series)
Captive Heroes - Book Six

··⁕··

A Hero's Welcome - Book One

Being injured and held captive isn't what astronaut Joe Hero had in
mind
when he agreed to explore a newly discovered planet for NASA.
But a man would have to be dead not to fall for the sexy female doctor
in charge of his care.
One night of scorching passion in the arms of the stranger
from another planet is enough to convince Annie that there's much
more to males
than she's been taught. Who is this sexy hunk and why does she feel
like
welcoming him into her bed every chance she gets?
Menu

A Hero Escapes - Book Two

Queen Jacey has always fantasized about bedding a male.
But taking one for her enjoyment is strictly forbidden. That is, until an
attractive well-hung stranger from another planet forces her to
overcome her training and her beliefs.
Being held captive and forced to mate with a gorgeous Queen isn't
exactly what astronaut Ben Hero expected when he agreed to explore a
newly discovered planet for NASA.
Escaping should be his top priority but making sizzling love to Jacey is
all he can think about.
When he discovers she's also being held against her will,
Ben's protective instincts kick in big time.
Suddenly they're on the run, irresistibly aroused, and wrapped in each
other's arms every chance they get!
Menu

A Hero Betrayed - Book Three

Astronaut Buck Hero didn't count on becoming infected with passion poison when he agreed to explore a newly discovered planet for NASA. If he doesn't get help soon he's going to be one very dead man. Fugitive on-the-run Virgin needs to decide whether to let the stranger die or administer the cure - a twenty-four-hour sex marathon. If he survives, she'll turn him over to his enemies and she'll gain her freedom. But her well-laid plans go into orbit when she discovers she's falling in love with her very well-hung patient.

A Hero's Kiss - Book Four

In Death Valley, the Boys rule and women are their slaves—each naked and bound to their captors' sexual desires.

Menu

A Hero's Kiss - Book Four

On a mission to the planet of Paradise in search of their missing brothers, US Astronaut Piper Hero and her two sisters become separated after crash-landing.

Infected by the deadly sensuous swamp water, Piper is tormented with arousing "fever sex dreams" and is rescued by the dangerously irresistible Jarod Ellis, who administers the lusty cure-wrenching climaxes that leave her breathless and so hot for sex she can't even think straight.

Finally free from his tortured life as a slave, Jarod Ellis has sworn never to trust a woman again. But he's instantly captivated by the sweet seductress Piper Hero, a women who claims to be related to the Earthmen he has vowed to protect with his life. Although he mistrusts her, she sets free untamed passions that scorch his body into an inferno of sexual needs.

Despite her own intimate fantasies coming true, Piper can't forget her mission of reuniting with her siblings and she'll do it—with or without the help of her well-hung stud.

Menu

• • ∞ • •

A Hero Needed - Book Five (Ellora's Cave)
Loosely connected with Pleasure Bound series
White picket fence-type, old-fashioned gal needs a man who loves to walk
in the rain. Must be well-hung. At least eight-inches long. Two inches
thick. Sharp green eyes. Clean-cut. Dark brown, short hair. A homebody,
white picket fence-type of guy. Sexual requirements—gentle yet untamed
lover. Sexually adventurous who will train to be same.
Must be romantic, enjoy sex toys, interested in mutual light bondage,
ménages are welcome.
That's what full-figured, antiques shop owner Jenna MacLean comes
up with when she and her best friend outline a want ad just for fun on
their weekly girls night out. When Jenna's ex-boyfriend, sexy Sully
Hero, decides he's the man in her ad, he's going to make all her
sizzling-hot fantasies come true.
After several years of being away from curvaceously sexy Jenna
MacLean, Sully's back in town and he's determined to get her back
into his bed—but he's not going through the traditional romantic
route. This time, he'll prove he loves her with help from the notorious
Ménage Club, a relationship club designed specifically to get estranged
couples back together with the help of a third and sometimes a
fourth...in the bedroom.
Menu

• • ❧ • •

Captive Heroes - Book Six (Ellora's Cave)
During a secret mission to locate their brothers on the faraway planet of
Paradise, the Hero sisters become separated after they crashland.
Taylor and Kayla
While searching for help, Kayla is bound and imprisoned by the
Breeders—along with a sexy male captive whose tantalizing scars
pique her interest. She's thankful when he rescues her, and irresistibly
aroused when she becomes his captive. Wild lust flares in Kayla's

eyes—an erotic side effect of the Fever Swamp water. Taylor is going to enjoy administering the cure—lots of sizzling hot sex!

Blackie and Kinley

Injured and lost in a dense jungle, Kinley is intimidated by the big, scarred man hot on her trail, especially considering the erotic power he holds over her. Capturing his beautiful female prey, Blackie can't wait to train her as a pleasure slave. When the well-hung male slips a collar around her neck, Kinley struggles with lust as a natural submissive.

<u>To Pleasure Bound Menu</u>

. . ⚜ . .

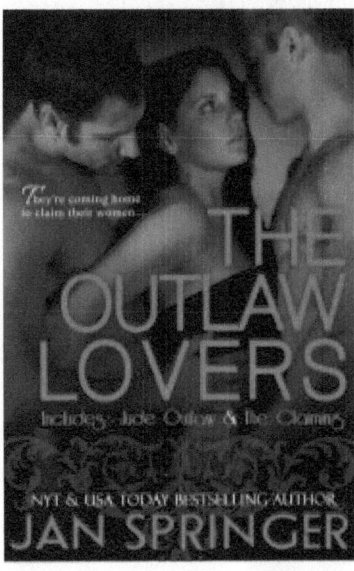

The Outlaw Lovers 2-book bundle
Jude Outlaw

(Outlaw Lovers 1)

A FAST-ACTING VIRUS has been unleashed, killing a vast majority of the world's female population, forcing the introduction of the Claiming Law. A law that states women are property that can only be claimed by groups of men...

When Cate Callahan learns Jude is coming home from the Terrorist Wars and is ready to claim her under the new law—with the help of his four brothers—she steals their boat and escapes to the high seas.

Unfortunately, her runaway bid for freedom doesn't last long.

Quickly capturing his lover, Jude rekindles the flames and seduces Cate back into his bed.

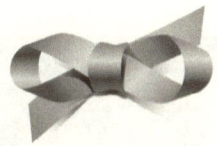

The Claiming

(Outlaw Lovers 2)
Seeking refuge from the Claiming Law, Callie Callahan hides in a
deserted cabin in the Maine woods and is shocked when her ex-flame
finds her. She's always craved being in Luke's arms.
Tasting him. Touching him. Loving him.
So, what's a girl to do but to delve into the sinful delights he offers...
Luke has finally reunited with the love of his life. There's only one way
to keep Callie safe and with him forever. He'll do it with the help of
his three brothers and some naughty toys. Rekindling the bright
flames between them, he unleashes Callie's sensual side with the
ultimate goal of introducing her to the Outlaw brothers...and the
Claiming.

.. ⚓ ..

Colter's Revenge (Outlaw Lovers 3)

In the near future, a virus has been unleashed killing a majority of the world's female population, forcing the introduction of the Claiming Law. A law that states men have all the rights and women are sexual property claimable by groups of men.

REVENGE BELONGS TO Dr. Colter Outlaw when he runs into the beautiful woman who broke his heart during the Terrorist Wars. Capturing her, collaring her and holding her against her will, he seduces her, fills her with wicked desires and cravings for a delicious ménage. Fully intent on breaking her heart and walking away, his plans unravel when he submits to the carnal pleasures Ashley gives him so freely...

He'd told her he loved her. Whispered promises of rescue from her life as a slave, then he'd disappeared. Infected with a version of the X-virus that leaves her sexually excited on a daily basis, Ashley Blakely has come to Pleasure Palace to bid on the cure. She never expected her

Outlaw Lover to screw her plans. Nor did she expect to give him her heart and body so easily...

Tyler's Woman (Outlaw Lovers 4)
In the near future, a virus has been unleashed, killing a majority of the world's female population, forcing the introduction of the Claiming Law. A law that states men have all the rights and women are sexual property claimable by groups of men.

LAURIE CALLAHAN HAS always experienced red-hot pleasure and passionate love in Tyler Outlaw's arms. But when he's pronounced MIA, presumed dead in the Terrorist Wars, her world is shattered and her heart broken.

For years, Tyler Outlaw and his best friend Hunter Brown endured brutal torture and worse in a terrorist prison. Finally free of their hell, they return home intent on seducing Laurie into their erotic-filled fantasies.

Shocked to discover Tyler is alive and he's taken a male lover, Laurie is thrust into a sensual world of sizzling seductions, scorching ménages and the carnal desires that both men crave. But she fears Tyler won't want her when he discovers she's not the same woman he left behind.

Reader Warning: Contains references to non-consensual sex.

Sensitive Readers may not wish to purchase this ebook. Please use discretion.

Resistance (Outlaw Lovers 5)

FUGITIVE FEMALE...

Renegade Resistance leader Reena Red Wilde is in for the fight of her life when she experiences an erotic attraction to the two most dangerous men she's ever met.

Black ops assassin...

Months ago, Will Blade Smith spent one sizzling evening in the arms of a red-haired seductress. Now she's his next assignment. One look into her gorgeous eyes and he's wrestling his heated cravings all over again.

Bounty Hunter...

When Cade Outlaw nabs his bounty, sexy-as-sin Reena Wilde, his profession dictates she's hands-off. But he can't ignore the magnetic sparks between them...or that she is the biggest temptation of his life.

Resistance is futile...

After Reena escapes Cade and Will and falls prey to a band of evil hunters, she's grateful her sexy hunks come to her rescue, and in return, saves their lives. Trapped in a solitary cabin during a wicked snowstorm, she can't resist her two well-hung studs, nor can she deny they've claimed her heart.

$$\bullet\ \bullet\ \cancel{\bullet}\ \bullet\ \bullet$$

THE DESPERADOES SERIES (Post-Catastrophic Erotic Romance Menage m/f/m/m)

A fiery eruption of solar flares disintegrates most of Earth's human population, frying electrical grids around the world and thrusting everyone into a cold, harsh land where only the strong survive...

The Pleasure Girl – Book One

Forced to become a pleasure girl in order to survive, Teyla Sutton reluctantly agrees to service dangerous desperado Logan Leigh and his two friends. White-hot pleasure becomes addictive beneath Logan's tender touches and his hard, muscular body. What Teyla never expected was to fall in love.

Logan knows he shouldn't allow the Pleasure Girl into his heart, but he also knows it's too late because she's already there. Soon three desperadoes are whisking Teyla away on an exquisite journey into her hottest dreams and forbidden desires. When she learns they are members of the notorious Durango Gang, can she allow them into her life, or will she send them away forever?

$$\bullet\ \bullet\ \cancel{\bullet}\ \bullet\ \bullet$$

IN HER BED – BOOK TWO

Before the Catastrophe, Dr. Elizabeth Brandywine would never have dreamed of actually surrendering to her wicked needs of being bound, dominated, and shared, but now there's no one left alive to judge her, except herself.

Ethan Durango knows sweet, uptight, sexy Dr. Liz is ready to submit to her secret sexual needs. Hes always wanted to share her. To have her tied up while he and his friends take her. Ethan, Landon, and Tyrell will enjoy seducing Liz past her boundaries until she submits to her naughtiest desires.

.. ᴄᴰ﹩ ..

BE MY DREAM TONIGHT – Book Three

Passionate ménages with the fierce men of the Durango gang have always made Eve Wright's body hum with sizzling arousal. Secretly, she loved all three men, that is, until she suffered a head injury and forgot them. Now her memory is returning with a carnal vengeance and she knows of only one way to relieve her sexual frustrations...by returning to the men she once loved.

When Eve shows up at their hideout, Kayne, Riley, and Maddox are pleased she wants them to help her remember what they once shared.

Their hot looks, tender touches, and scorching pleasure-pain leaves Eve tangled in an erotic storm that threatens to break her heart and give up a gut-wrenching secret.

.. ᴄᴰ﹩ ..

NEWSLETTER

Hi! If you would like to get an email when my books are released, you can sign up here:

Newsletter: http://ymlp.com/xguembmugmgb

Your emails will never be shared and you can unsubscribe whenever you like.

•• ⚬⚮⚬ ••

ABOUT THE AUTHOR

Jan Springer writes full-time at her home nestled in cottage country, Ontario, Canada. She enjoys hiking, kayaking, gardening, reading and writing. She is a member of the Writers Union of Canada, Romance Writers of America. She loves hearing from her readers.

•• ⚬⚮⚬ ••

A WORD FROM THE AUTHOR

Hi! Thank you for purchasing this book. Word of mouth is important for any author to succeed. If you enjoyed this story feel free to leave a short review at the place where you bought it. I would really appreciate it. I look forward to bringing you more stories in the near future.

If you would like to contact me or personally send me feedback, you can reach me at janspringerauthor@gmail.com

.. ᴏᴘ ..

HERE ARE OTHER WAYS we can connect:

.. ᴏᴘ ..

JAN SPRINGER WEBSITE at http://www.janspringer.com
Facebook - https://www.facebook.com/janspringereroticromance
Tsu - https://www.tsu.co/janspringer
Twitter - https://twitter.com/janspringer @janspringer
Pinterest - http://www.pinterest.com/janspringer1/
Jan's Blog - http://janspringerauthor.wordpress.com/blog-2/
LinkedIn: http://ca.linkedin.com/in/janspringerauthor/
Google   Plus   -   https://plus.google.com/u/0/101527334949931513035/posts
Jan's Newsletter: http://ymlp.com/xguembmugmgb
Spunky Girl Publishing: http://spunkygirlpublishing.com
Goodreads: https://www.goodreads.com/author/show/260628.Jan_Springer

Don't miss out!

Visit the website below and you can sign up to receive emails whenever Jan Springer publishes a new book. There's no charge and no obligation.

https://books2read.com/r/B-A-WGQ-KKMF

BOOKS 2 READ

Connecting independent readers to independent writers.

Also by Jan Springer

Pleasure Bound
A Hero's Welcome
A Hero Escapes
A Hero Betrayed
A Hero's Kiss
A Hero Wanted
Captive Heroes

Pleasure Bound Boxed Set
Pleasure Bound : COMPLETE SERIES SciFi Erotic Romance Boxed Set

Tentacles Shifter Erotic Romance
Taken by Him

The Key Club
A Merry Menage Christmas
Sophie's Menage
Jewel's Menage
Jaxie's Menage

The Outlaw Lovers
Jude Outlaw
The Claiming

Colter's Revenge
Tyler's Woman
Resistance
The Outlaw Lovers
Alpha Outlaws Boxed Set

Vampira

Sweet Heat
Dark Heat
Wet Heat
Crimson Heat

Standalone

A Touch of Menage Boxed Set
Shades of Menage Boxed Set
Nice Girl Naughty
Sinderella Sexy
The Biker and The Bride
The Fire Within
Bared to Him
Pleasure Bound : A Futuristic Adult Romance Boxed Set
Merry Menage Kisses Boxed Set
Inner Girl Rising
Stripped Naked
Risqué Girl Delights Boxed Set
A Holiday Menage
Ménage À Trois
A Hitman for Hannah
Billionaire Boyfriend
Edible Delights

Vampira
Toygasm
The Dark Side

Watch for more at www.janspringer.com.